MJ Miller

All About Annie

© Copyright 2019 MJ Miller

All rights reserved. This book or any portion thereof may not be reproduced or used in any manner whatsoever without the express written permission of the publisher except for the use of brief quotations in a book review. Thank you for respecting the work of this author.

This is a work of fiction. Names, characters, places, and incidents either are the products of the author's imagination or are used fictitiously. Any resemblance to actual persons, living or dead, businesses, companies, events, or locales is entirely coincidental.

ISBN: 9781080368013

Acknowledgements

Huge huge thanks go to Maria for her dedication to helping me realize my dreams. To Emily for her eagle eye and warding off typos. To Kathy for being my biggest critic. To Melissa for putting up with my constant out loud plot twists. To Ann for the expert editorial review. And none of this would be possible without the support of my fabulous better half, Doug and his willingness to binge watch ridiculous reality shows with me to unwind.

For Eric.

Chapter 1

Annie closed the door and leaned her back up against it and rolled her eyes. It was always like this. Every date she'd been on in the last, oh, 5 years or so. And there weren't all that many. Reasonably okay looking guys with reasonably okay personalities and absolutely no chemistry whatsoever. Usually fix ups. Because everyone and their mother, and their aunt, and their next-door neighbor wanted to see Annie find a guy. And they all had the perfect one in mind. Only none of them were. And they never would be. Not that she even needed the perfect guy or any guy at this point.

It was futile and she knew it. At 35, her biological clock was ticking so loud it made a sonic boom seem like a tap. At this rate those 6 kids she thought she'd have was already down to 3 at best. Glancing at the clock, the real one on the wall, she sighed. It was only 9:00. Nine O'Clock on a Friday night, in the world's greatest city, and she was already home from another fun-filled date. Any other sane woman would be just heading out after spending hours on her hair and makeup, honing her flirting skills in the mirror. Not Annie.

She never was very good at being anyone other than herself. She wasn't elegant and refined, like her sister. Instead Annie was definitely down to earth with a killer sense of humor. She simply wasn't into the glitzy nightlife. She wasn't comfortable in the bohemian part of town either, maybe she wasn't eclectic enough. She just didn't seem to fit. Which in New York is kind of virtually impossible. Everyone fits. Except Annie. She belonged in an adorable little house with a white picket fence in a small coastal town with a bunch of kids and an amazing, devoted, faithful husband who would love her till the day she died and beyond.

That's what Annie wanted. Which is most likely why Annie was never satisfied. Not with her job. Not with the guys she met. Not with her life in general. She was constantly reinventing herself in her mind and imagining what would, or should, happen next. And every one of her daydreams and fantasies took her to the same impossible place. She knew it wasn't ever to be. She'd had the same fantasy play out over and over since she was 18. The details would change. The circumstances would be different. But always, always she ended up with him in that perfect house in that quintessential little town on the ocean.

Annie gazed out across her living room. Just one more part of her life that was completely out of sync. She'd tried to decorate it right out of an HGTV show. Her gentrified brownstone apartment was meant to be urban rustic contemporary but somehow it just ended up looking like someone delivered the wrong furniture. Interior decorating was just not her thing. Sighing, she crossed over to the way-too-overstuffed sofa, and grabbed the book lying there. She'd barely gotten through the first few chapters, not that it wasn't good. It was great. And Annie loved to read. She could sit and read all day if she didn't have to actually go to work to pay the rent. Losing herself in a good book was the next best thing to losing herself to her fantasies. Any good therapist would tell her she needed serious help to confront her escapist personality, but Annie enjoyed it too much. She was perfectly content to live another life in her head. The life that simply must include a devastatingly charming, handsome lover. She flipped open the page she'd dog-eared and continued to read on.

Cliffside was, at first glance, a seemingly quiet, picturesque lakeside town in northeast Ohio. Nestled on the banks of Lake Erie, it had remained true, steadfast, for centuries. Through natural disasters, like the 100-year flood back in '69. Through man-made tragedies, like the Great Depression. It had remained as it ever was. Seeming to renew itself year after year through the lives of its residents. Perhaps it fed itself off their hopes and dreams. Loves and losses. Most of the townspeople were fourth, fifth, even sixth generation Siders, as they were known. The children grew into adulthood, and took their turns venturing outside the town limits. Some for a short while, to attend school or explore parts unknown. Others to seek their fortune. But most eventually came back to settle. That's just how it always was. And always would be.

Now that's my kind of town, thought Annie. Closing her eyes briefly, she imagined herself standing atop a rocky cliff looking out over the sea, waiting for her lover to sail home.

All About Annie

Sheriff Colby had done it. Gone off to college to study criminal justice. Took him 6 years. He'd worked his way through, as did most Siders who chose college. Cliffside wasn't a poor town, nor a rich one. It was mostly working folks. Too far from the city to attract the Cleveland commuters, the small smattering of affluence was attributed mostly to old money, the kind that had always been there. Northsiders. Those that lived just north of the highway that ran through town. Their tasteful, rustic homes were invisible to the passing traffic, tucked away amidst the wooded and ragged coastline.

Sheriff Max Colby grew up south of the highway, but protecting the Northsiders was just as much his job as anything else. And when the call came in for a disturbance at the Helms house, he didn't waste time getting out there. He was off duty, but none of his three deputies were able to handle it. Or maybe he was unwilling to let them. Either way, he felt he owed it to his major campaign donor, Gwen Helms Forsythe, to check it out personally.

Pulling into the long, winding drive that led to the main house, the Sheriff glanced around uneasily. Something didn't fit. Nothing looked unusual, but it was dark, and the only light was the moon casting its glow, throwing shadows among the trees. Viola Hammond had called in frantically 15 minutes earlier. Said she'd heard screams coming from the main house. Viola was the Helms housekeeper and had been for over 35 years. She lived in a small cottage on the edge of the property. Gwen had moved her there when she'd gotten married. The first time. Viola was known to have quite the imagination, and was virtually the sole source of all town gossip, but something in her voice made him take notice this time. She sounded desperate, not chatty. The house was dark, and quiet. It was large; more of a manor than a house, and it had stood on the rocky cliff overlooking the lake for over 200 years. Built of stone, it was 3 stories tall, and just as wide. An imposing structure, when it was dark, it was truly eerie. Even for Max Colby.

Getting out of his truck, he paused, his hand resting on his gun, tucked neatly in his side holster. He felt a prickle on the back of his neck and tuned into that gut instinct he'd always been famous for. From the time he was just a small boy, he had an uncanny knack for sensing things. Everyone in Cliffside knew it, which was probably why they chose him for Sheriff to begin with.

He approached the front entrance carefully, glancing around as he did so. The large stone pillars were set widely apart, creating the appearance of a grand entryway. Usually the 1790s streetlamp replicas in front of the pillars were glowing softly, but they were off. As was every light in the house. First sign of trouble, thought Max. Gwen was a nervous woman, and usually the house was lit up like a Christmas tree all night long.

He climbed the steps, still looking around cautiously. As he approached the massive wood entry door, he stopped suddenly. It was open, just a crack. Gwen had the door locked at all times. Maybe he should call for back up, or maybe he was just overreacting. Nope. This was trouble. Big trouble. Pulling his radio from his pocket, he backed himself down the steps, and spoke quietly to Reagan, his dispatcher. "Get Tony, Mike and John down here now. Tell them there's trouble down here at Gwen's. Tell them to keep the sirens off and come in the back way. I'm out front. I'll meet 'em there."

Oh for god's sake, thought Annie, *what's he look like? I can't envision a character without some description. How annoying, leaving all the good stuff out.* "Typical," she murmured to herself. She began reading again, and noted the change in scene. Always a sign a new character was coming into play.

"Hot damn!" She swore as she put down the newspaper. Gwen Helms. Aka Gwen Forsythe, aka Gwen Talbot. Suicide. Jade couldn't believe it.

"Aha!" Annie spoke out loud, which, living alone, had become a habit. "The heroine's name is Jade! How prophetic." Annie rolled her eyes. "I'll just put my own image in there. Small, no petite. Light brown hair. Nope, let's make that *golden* brown hair. Big expressive eyes. Cute, not sophisticated. OK that works." She sighed. She still couldn't picture the Sheriff.

Jade's journalistic instincts told her something wasn't right with this story. Not right at all. Of course she hadn't gotten past the headline yet, 'Ohio's grande dame of society commits suicide.' Jade picked up the paper and scanned through the article.

'Found with empty prescription bottle still in hand.' Oh please, thought Jade. Like she collapsed immediately after swallowing the pills. 'Depressed following recent break up of marriage.' Gimme a break! 'Always seeking attention.' Actually, that's true. No note. If she knew Gwen, and she did, there'd have been a 200-page letter. What kind of dumb-ass investigation was this? She scanned the article again, and dropped the paper as if it burned to the touch.

Sheriff Colby. Sheriff Max Colby. It couldn't be. No way. No fucking way. Jade took a deep breath and shook her head. God she needed a drink. Something. Her body was tensing up and she suddenly felt as if she'd stuck her finger in a socket. Jolts of electricity just humming through her veins. Max. Her sweet, beautiful Max.

"Now we're getting somewhere," said Annie.

Her friend Max. Although she'd never seen him quite as a friend. That was his take on their relationship, not hers. She'd fantasized at least once a day, every day, for the last 10 years reliving those times with him. What could she have done differently? No. More like who could she have been that would have made him notice her. Actually, he did notice her. He just didn't make a pass at her. Ever. She could have walked across the room naked and he wouldn't have blinked. Not that she ever went that far. Unrequited love. And for Jade, it had lived with her for far too long. It was a schoolgirl crush for christ's sake. Well, college schoolgirl crush anyway. But her feelings were so strong, so deep, she'd never gotten rid of them. Never moved on.

"You and me both! I know just how you feel, girl." Annie was really into the character now.

Seeing his name in print made him real again. It made her feel again. She felt like screaming. So she did. AAAAAAAAAAAAGH. There that was better. Her neighbors probably heard that. She screamed again for good measure. They wouldn't say anything. Nobody ever said anything in her building. The old brownstone was one of dozens lining the boulevard in her uptown Manhattan neighborhood. A quiet, sedentary neighborhood where everyone nodded their greetings, but rarely spoke more than 2 words to each other. Everyone busy with their own little lives. Caught up in their own little dramas. Not wanting to care about anyone else's. It wasn't what she'd wanted. What she'd hoped for.

Annie put the book down and sighed. Then frowned. Then sighed again. Then scrunched her face up in a curious look. It was as if he was writing about her. Not the journalist part, unless you actually considered ad copy journalism, but she did recognize herself. Parts of her anyway. Maybe she shouldn't keep reading. Maybe whatever happens will make her depressed, or maybe give her hope? Keep reading. That's the only way to find out. She picked up the book and curled up in the corner of her sofa. It was Friday after all; no work tomorrow, she could sit and read all night if she wanted to.

Yawning, and straining to open her eyes, she glanced at the clock and saw it was past 3am. She opened her eyes wide in a kind of stretching exercise, hoping they'd stay open that way. She couldn't go to bed now, she was halfway through with the book and couldn't possibly put it down. This guy had hit too close to home on so many levels, she had to finish it. Was her life so ordinary, so common, that this guy could write a bestseller and include all her thoughts and emotions without even knowing her? Were so many other women out there suffering the same existence? *One more chapter,* she thought, *and I'll go to bed. Maybe.*

Emotions roared through him. She could still make him feel like a teenager in heat. He'd loved her from the start. He never had a chance to fall in love slowly, or suffer the heartbreak of loss. It was as if he plunged in an instant, and never came up for air.

He turned away, not wanting, nor allowing his emotions to be seen or felt. He walked over to his truck, opened the door, climbed in and started her up. He knew he was out of control when he heard his tires screech as he floored it. Escape. He had to escape. He sped out the long drive and hit the highway blacktop with a bounce and thud. Easing up on the accelerator, he took a deep breath, then another one. Calm down! He screamed inside his head. He swerved suddenly to avoid the cottontail in the road, who'd eyed him with nothing but curiosity. Damn bunny he thought. Taking another deep breath, he felt starved for oxygen. Pull over! Yeah. Pull over. That's what he needed to do, and did. Swerving off the highway onto the shoulder, he stopped short and cut the engine. Leaning his head back he closed his eyes and tried to shut out the flood of memories, but it was futile. She was here. Here. She was here! The image of her face, her deep expressive eyes, the soft, kissable lips. Thoughts swam through his head.

He'd have to go back, he knew that. Not yet. He needed to collect his thoughts. Calm down, and brace himself. He knew his life was about to change. He just couldn't figure out how.

Annie hadn't even known she'd fallen asleep. Waking up so suddenly startled her. The book lay open on her lap. The phone. Damnit, that's what was causing all the noise. Right now she was regretting her choice of ringtone. Sounded like a screaming banshee. Now, where was that phone? She almost jumped up, but stopped herself, and instead carefully placed the book on the coffee table, almost reverently, as if parting from it was almost painful. Realizing the noise was coming from somewhere nearby, she searched around the sofa cushions till she found it and quickly answered.

"Hello?"

"Hi there ducky! Rise and shine!"

Annie groaned, very dramatically, to make a point.

"Hey sis. Little early for this, don't you think? Especially since you know I was out last night with that charmer you set me up with."

"Precisely why I'm calling. So how'd it go? Cute, huh?"

"I suppose."

"And?"

"And what?"

"I'm coming over. I need to hear everything."

"Yeah, of course you do. Whatever." Annie hung up and sighed. There was no way she could deal with Luce right now but there was no way to stop her.

She surveyed the room, then looked down. She hadn't even changed out of her "date" clothes. Boy would her sister get the wrong idea. Annie smiled wickedly. Wouldn't that be a kick! She could have some fun here with this. Anything to liven up her day. She was grinning now. *Let the games begin*!

She started to hum as she snuggled back down with the book. No sense getting dressed now.

Max kept his eyes closed as his breathing became steadier. The horrible pit in his stomach seemed to just grow bigger and more painful. All those years had gone by, and yet when she'd looked up at him, it seemed time had just stood still. Oh she was a little older, a little curvier, but it didn't matter. It had never mattered. From the first moment he'd seen her, standing in the doorway on that long-ago evening, he'd been captured. She'd come in with a friend, and the party was being held in a small room on campus. Most seats were taken already, and there was a crowd of students practically standing on top of each other. So she had paused, scanning the room for a clear area. He'd looked up from his perch in the corner, and had caught her glance as it passed over. They'd stared at each other for what seemed like an eternity. She'd smiled. He'd smiled.

After a moment's hesitation she came into the room, and spotted a seat near him. She'd sat down quickly, smiled at him once more, then began the greeting ritual so common at these informal parties. Finally Rick, the host and his best friend, had come over and introduced them. Without a second thought, he'd gotten up and decided to sit next to her. He wasn't subtle or casual about it either. He felt like a piece of metal being pulled by a magnet. She turned her head as he sat down and smiled at him one more time. That was it. They'd spent the next 5 hours talking. About what he'd never remember. He hadn't really been listening anyway, just watching her lips move as she spoke. They were soft and red, naturally. Her skin was fair, like peaches and cream. No makeup.

No pretenses. Her soft golden brown hair hung long past her shoulders. Her eyes were enormous pools with little flecks that seemed to sparkle like gold.

"Ha! See, golden brown. I knew it," Annie announced to herself.

He could tell she wasn't very tall. Probably wasn't more than 5'3 or so. And even at 18, she had the curves that so many girls were missing. He didn't much care for stick figures, and she was filled out in all the right places. Too soon his ride told him it was time to hit the road. He'd gotten up, smiled down at her, and said goodbye. Didn't get her number. Didn't get her last name. He'd been a complete fool.

The next time he saw her he'd been an even bigger fool. He'd been visiting a friend in her building, and gone upstairs to see if he could find her. Rick had filled him in on who she was and where she lived. He got lucky. She was headed out of the shower room and in the hall. He could have let her just go into her room unnoticed since she was dressed in nothing but a skimpy towel, but no. He did what any fool would do and called out her name and waved. She'd glanced over, and he realized too late the look on her face was pure embarrassment. She smiled weakly and gave a little half wave, then practically dove into her room. She didn't come back out, though he waited for quite a while. Who could blame her?

"No no no no no no." Annie whispered in horror. "This is soooo not happening."

CHAPTER 2

"Annie! Hey! Annie!"

Annie closed her eyes and opened them again. Squinting, she realized she was looking at Luce.

"What the hell are you doing here?" she demanded.

"Well, gee sis, you don't answer the door, I have to break in using the key you keep hidden where anyone can find it, and then I come in and you're sitting here catatonic."

"So, what, I fell asleep. So sue me."

"Your eyes were wide open! You were dazed, comatose. Out of your head!"

"Sorry," Annie replied sheepishly, and tried a light grin to ease the mood. "I was reading this book, and this is gonna sound weird, but I think it's about me."

"Come again?"

"I said," Annie continued quietly, "that it's about me. Do me a favor and pour me a glass of Zin, would you?"

"Annie, it's a little early, don't you think?" Luce was used to Annie's overreacting to things, but this was not the usual.

"Just pour it, OK?"

"You got it." Whatever it was, Luce figured, she would talk her down from it. She always did. She swung around on her heels and headed for the small kitchen. She was Annie's opposite in every way. They may have been sisters, but there was no resemblance. Not in looks, or personality. Even though it was Saturday morning, and Luce had no plans, she was dressed impeccably. A short black pencil skirt accentuated her long legs, and the turquoise silk blouse brought out the blue in her eyes. She was tall, slim and elegant. Everything Annie wasn't.

Luce came back with the wine, and eyed Annie closely.

"Must have been some date, you're still in your 'date' clothes." Luce grinned.

"Huh? Oh, yeah, some date." Annie had forgotten all about the little trick she had planned. She'd forgotten all about the date for that matter.

"OK. What are you reading that's got you so spooked?"

Annie handed the book to Luce.

"Oh my god!" exclaimed Luce with a rush. "It's the new C.A. McLain book. I've been dying to read this. It just came out. I get first dibs when you're done!"

"Whatever." Annie picked up her wine glass and threw back her head, drinking it all down in one big gulp.

Luce turned to look at Annie. "So the book's about you, eh?" she said with a smile.

"Yes." Annie looked up at her sister, and Luce could tell there was no humor in her eyes. Her face looked almost ghostly.

"Care to explain why C.A. McLain, reclusive bestselling author, would be writing about you?"

"Don't know. But he is."

"I hate to break it to you sis, but you and 10,000 other women. Yesterday morning we got another 500 emails at the station from women claiming to be his muse. And now you too, huh?"

Annie eyed her sister curiously. "So, I'm not the only one who thinks this book is about her, huh? How ordinary my life must be, when someone writes my biography and everyone else claims it's theirs."

"Well, maybe I better read it. I won't take long, and I promise I'll give it back."

"No."

"What do you mean, no?"

"No. I am keeping this book forever. No one will touch it. It's my story, don't you see?" Annie was sounding petulant now, and Luce was frustrated.

"Annie be reasonable. You don't know C.A. McLain. Why would he write about you?" As much as Luce adored her sister, she couldn't fathom why anyone with C.A. McLain's money and fame would write about her. She wasn't glamorous or extraordinary, after all. Sweet, sure, and lovable, but not the type to attract the attention of a best-selling author. Luce suddenly felt guilty for thinking that way. Pretty shallow. No one knew anything at all about this guy, and maybe Annie was his type.

"I don't know that I don't know him," Annie replied somewhat harshly. She became more animated "No one knows who he is right? You told me yourself he writes under an assumed name? You wanted him on the entertainment segment remember? But you can't find him?"

"Yeah, that's right."

Annie stood up and started pacing across the room. "How do we know that I don't know him? Maybe he's someone I knew a long time ago. What I do know is everything in this book seems to be about us. Like it could have come straight from my journal… say Luce, is there something you want to tell me?" Annie stopped short, turned and eyed her sister suspiciously.

"Don't be absurd. What do you mean 'us'? You and me? Or, like a couple?"

"No, us like a couple of friends. That's what we were. Friends. Now go away, get your own copy of the book, then we'll talk. I'm going to bed."

"It's 9 in the morning. And you still haven't answered my question. Who else is it about Annie?"

"Nobody. It's about nobody," Annie repeated, and swung around and headed into her bedroom, slamming the door behind her. Luce stood and stared at the closed door for a moment, her brows crinkling. She'd have to go get a copy of the book and see just what was in it that was making Annie so paranoid.

By Sunday night, Annie had finished the book. Her head had been reeling all weekend. The whole thing was too much. She knew, without a doubt, who C.A. McLain was writing about. What she couldn't understand was how he'd written about her so intuitively, as if he'd known what she thought, how she felt. It had to be somebody close to her. Maybe C.A.

wasn't even a man. Maybe a woman? Someone she knew back then. Maybe this was some sort of twisted gift from the past. Some friend she'd lost touch with. Or, god forbid, a stalker.

Or maybe Luce was right. Maybe the author was tapping into every woman's fantasy, that the one they love loves them back. Maybe she was just like everyone else, but the coincidences were just too spot on really. The scenes too detailed, like they were ripped from her long-ago memories. Or maybe she was just somehow altering her memories to fit the book. It's possible. She'd taken enough psych courses to understand the phenomenon. But the anxiety running through her made her wonder anyway.

She let the phone ring 6 times before answering. She knew it was Luce, that banshee ringtone a dead giveaway, and got an inward pleasure from making her wait.

"Hey, Luce" Annie tried to sound normal, no easy feat.

"Hey, Annie, listen. I read the book. I'm coming over." Luce never waited for a response; she knew Annie wasn't going anywhere, not that it would stop her.

"Never mind it Luce. I figured it out and you're right. I'm just like everyone else. Hopelessly daydreaming that I could be someone's truly madly deeply. How many emails did the station get this weekend?"

"Another thousand, plus the phone calls and tweets. Totally irrelevant. Listen, Annie. This guy is writing about someone in his life. And I have to admit, some of the dialogue is definitely in character for you. Some of the things that Jade… I mean really, Jade? Some of the things she does would be *just* like you. And then there's the shower scene. Remember you called me in the middle of the night to cry in embarrassment?"

"I also remember it happened to like 10 other girls on my floor that same semester, kind of a given in a dorm. At least now you see why I said it's all about me, but now I also see how it could be a thousand other women!" Annie sighed.

"Did you read the end?"

"Well duh."

"Really read it. Like really, really read it?"

"Yes Luce, I really, *really* read it." Annie's voice held a note of defeat.

"He's calling out to her, Annie. He's asking her to take a chance. The one she… YOU… didn't take before."

"So what's your point?" Annie knew where this was going and she did NOT want to go there at all.

"My point is, that if it is you, we need to figure this out. I'm coming over."

She heard the click and let out a huge breath. She couldn't really handle any of this. Yeah she'd read the ending. About a hundred times.

> *"Why didn't you tell me?"*
> *"Tell you what Max?"*
> *"How you really felt."*
> *"Oh I don't know, fear of rejection? Or maybe it was you and that bimbo on your lap at the tavern? Let me think about it and I'll get back to you."*

"You should have told me Jade," Max was frustrated now.

"And you should have told me, Max!" Jade retorted, equally frustrated.

"I'm telling you now," Max spoke almost pleadingly.

"What, Max, what are you telling me now?"

"That it's you. It's always been you." There. He'd said it. Now it was up to Jade.

He waited, eyes focused on her like laser beams.

"Well then," she answered, nodding, her face almost expressionless. Unreadable. *"I'll take it under advisement."* And with that, she turned and walked away. Leaving him hanging, as she always had, he thought.

Jade kept walking, picking up the pace. Just this once, she thought, she was going to make Max Colby suffer as she had all this time. She would tell him of course. Just not here, and not now. But soon enough, she'd tell him the truth.

Annie felt like she was in a Groundhog Day episode of the Twilight Zone. Reliving one of the most painful memories she had. The nerve of this guy. Writing a book and making a buck at the expense of her sanity! Now Annie was hungry, in fact almost starved. Anger seemed to get her appetite going. But she'd have to wait for Luce to leave before actually eating. Luce only lived a block away, so she couldn't wolf anything worthy down before she got there. Luce's idea of dinner was usually some smelly fish with a side of salad made of leaves and twigs, while Annie could suck down a package of Twinkies as a main course without a second thought.

She heard the buzzer, and called for Luce to come in.

"What's with the buzzer? Don't you knock anymore?"

"Nah, you never answer when I do." Luce breezed in and made herself at home on the sofa.

"So what is this earth-shattering discussion going to cover?" Annie asked a bit dryly. She knew her sister was up to something.

"It's simple. Just tell me which parts of the book make you think it's you. I know which ones I'd pick out as red flags, but what struck you first? Aside from the name Jade of course…"

Annie smiled at Luce, a gleam in her eye as she spoke.

"All of it."

"Come on Annie, I need details!"

"I mean it, Luce, all of it. Every last bit of it. Except for the fictional murder and all that."

"Give me an example," Luce demanded.

"No!" Annie replied a bit too emphatically.

"Come on!" Luce's voice was impatient.

"Look, Annie, the character fits you to a tee. Even I could see that."

"Yeah but the author could be anyone. Anyone that knew me," Annie replied.

"All right then. That guy you mooned over in college. You think he's the guy in the book? Max Colby? Wasn't he the one that caught you in your towel, the infamous shower scene?"

"Yes," her faced reddened at the memory. Annie rolled her eyes. "And it wasn't a shower scene, this isn't a remake of Psycho," she added.

"How about the scene where he meets her the first time. Sound familiar?" Luce asked.

"Luce really, lots of people meet like that at college parties."

"And the pizza delivery guy?"

Annie rolled her eyes again. "OMG yes," remembering the moment she discovered the guy she was chatting away with downstairs wasn't her blind date after all.

"But Luce, college students? Pizza? Dorms? Mistaken identity? All common!"

"Are you still mooning over him?" Luce knew the answer, but asked anyway.

"Yeah," Annie sighed. *Always*, she thought.

"Then that settles it."

"Luce, I've thought about it and I know I'm nuts, okay? Don't you think half the guys in the universe have seen a girl in her towel? Or met one at a party? It's not those things. It's the feelings. It's the way he describes how Jade felt about it all. Whoever wrote this had to have some pretty intimate knowledge of my personal life." Annie still wasn't sure whether she should be excited about this or terrified.

"I think C.A. McLain wrote you a love story. That's what I think." Luce smiled knowingly at her sister. She was actually beginning to warm up to the idea that her baby sister was a muse.

"Then the question is… who is C.A. McLain?" Annie asked.

"Why your secret love. That's obvious!" Luce laughed. Time for some tension reduction the room was so thick with it.

"Him? An author? Come on get real. Look, it's possible C.A. is someone I went to college with. Probably a good enough acquaintance to know the dirt, but not good enough for me to keep in touch with." Annie's brain was in high gear now. "Maybe it's Sam?"

"Sam?" Luce hadn't heard her mention a Sam before.

Annie ignored Luce, lost in her train of thought. "Damnit! This is insane. It's not about me. Okay. Please Luce, no more. You'll have me start believing this shit is real again, and I don't like real. I like make-believe. In fact, let me just live out my days holding onto this one little fantasy. I'll go to my grave believing that a bestselling author was secretly madly in love with me. Nuf said."

"What does Jen say?" Luce figured by now Annie had told her good friend.

"I don't know I haven't spoken to her about it. And before you say a word, I'm not going to."

"Fine, you will, but moving on, get some paper. We need to make a list." Luce stood up and looked about for something to write on.

"What kind of list?"

"Names, sis. Anyone you can think of that knew about your secret passion and was around for most of the incidents that appear in the book."

"So that's what, like the other three thousand fellow students that attended when I did?" Annie stood up, intending to usher her sister straight out the door,

"Don't be silly. Just the people who knew both of you. You and your hottie."

"Don't call him that."

"Hottie hottie hottie."

"Shut up Luce."

"Just give me the names," Luce commanded.

Luce found a legal pad as Annie sighed and sat back down on the couch, knowing there was no stopping Luce at this point. Propping her feet up, and tapping her chin with her fingertip, she played along, rattling off a list of friends from college that might fit the characters in the book, or might have known them.

When Annie finally said "That's it," Luce breathed a sigh of relief. "OK, then, we've got a lot of names here. We'll need to eliminate. After we add one more."

"One more?"

"Yep. Your hunk. What was his name, anyway, I don't even remember anymore."

Annie sighed. "Chris, And I told you, it wasn't him. It isn't him. He's not a writer. Not that he couldn't be, but this book wasn't written by him, no way!" Annie made a huffing sound and folded her arms across her chest.

"Come on Annie, how do you know? Chris? See, it begins with a C, so what's his middle name?"

Annie's eyes widened.

"Well?" Luce was impatiently drumming her fingers on the edge of the sofa.

"Um, Asa."

"C.A., well what do you know." Luce smiled wickedly. "Guess he secretly harbored all those feelings for you and you just didn't know."

Annie remained silent. Her face had a sudden drawn, ashen look to it.

"I don't want to do this Luce. I don't want to know, I just want to forget the whole thing."

"Is it that painful?" Luce suddenly felt a pang of sympathy. What had started out as just a fun fantasy was really doing a number on her sister, and she didn't want to hurt her.

Annie didn't answer, so Luce got up, ripped the paper off the pad, folded it and tucked it in her purse. "We'll drop it for now, Annie. I'm going shopping. I'll call you later."

CHAPTER 3

C.A. McLain stood in the doorway and looked around. The cabin was just as he'd left it, albeit a little more dust than usual. *Being gone for a month would do that*, he thought. But it felt so good to be back. And now, with the book finished, and well on its way to number one, he hoped, he'd finally be able to relax up here. He shivered, and realized how cold the cabin was. He needed to get busy. The firewood stack was completely depleted. He could see the cobwebs were starting to appear around the window complete with their spiny little inhabitants. Pulling the covers off the furniture he breathed in the cloud of dust. *Shit!* It would take him hours if not days to get this place clean. He should have hired a caretaker. Or at the very least just had someone stop in once a week. He shook his head and chuckled. *Fame and fortune... right?* "Guess even celebrity authors have chores to do!" he mused to himself. He shrugged his shoulders, sighed, and then with no alternative, got busy with the tasks at hand.

It took a bit more than a few hours, but in the end the place once again looked cozy and comfortable. The kind of place they could have shared together. "Damn" he whispered softly. *She's still with me. Maybe,* he thought, *she always will be.*

He strode purposefully into the kitchen and poured himself a very tall Scotch. Taking a large swig, he shuddered. He didn't drink this stuff too often. Now he knew why. He set the glass down with a thud. His six foot plus frame filled the tiny room with its 7-foot ceiling. He had to duck under the exposed wooden beams just to get to the fridge. Yanking open the door, he grabbed one of the small deli containers he'd brought along, retrieved his glass, ducked back out into the great room, and sat back down on the sofa. Putting his feet up on the old wooden table, he made quick work of the salad and tossed the container and fork on the table. It wasn't much, but he'd do some grocery shopping at the local market tomorrow and stock up. His list was growing. Firewood. Food. Beer, because this Scotch was disgusting. He only had it in the cabin because his buddies liked it. Leaning back, he closed his eyes and tried to blank out his thoughts. Sipping his drink, making a face, sipping again. He breathed for relaxation. Yeah, the book was done but the haunting wasn't. He didn't want to think of her. Not now. He looked over at the windowsill, at the photo sitting there. Mocking him. Painfully tugging at him. He'd made mistakes. Big ones. But she was the biggest.

He remembered the day he took the photo. They'd gone to the lake to celebrate the end of the semester. A few dozen college students in high spirits caravanning up to their favorite spot by a rocky jetty on the lake. Some of the couples had taken off for a long "walk" but the two of them just spent the time talking. About everything it seemed. And they'd innocently flirted back and forth. He could still see the laughter on her face when he'd made some stupid joke that no one would have laughed at. But she did. When she'd gone to stretch her legs, he'd grabbed the camera on a whim and snapped the photo of her, standing at the end of the jetty looking out over the lake. He'd zoomed in, and had been suddenly struck by the look on her face. As if she were waiting for something, or someone. It was his lost moment, he knew that now.

The awareness had come to him when he began writing his latest novel. He had felt the vision start to take shape the way it always does just before he starts writing. Only this time, it wasn't his genre at all. This one was romance all the way, and since he was no romance writer he struggled to identify what the hell was going on. His readers demanded mystery and intrigue. But his soul seemed to demand he write about her.

In the end, it became a story within a story. It had mystery. Intrigue. And *her*.

It had taken only 2 months. In fact it seemed to have written itself. As opposed to the year he spent on his last novel writing each chapter and rewriting each chapter over and over. When he was through, he thought he'd finally cleansed his soul of her and without even a figurative backward glance he wrote a brief email and sent it off to his editor.

Only now, sitting here in the cabin, chilled to the bone, endlessly staring at her photo, he realized his mistake. You can't just write someone out of your life.

#######

Mark Simeon leaned back in his chair and clasped his hands behind his head. A smile played upon his face as, reading the latest reviews, he realized his favorite client had once again come through. Big time. But Mark had sensed a difference this time. This was a book written from the heart, and he knew it. The author's emotions were clearly out there for all to see. His books had always been good, his style tight. But the one thing C.A. McLain had been criticized for in the past was the lack of depth and emotion in his novels.

Not this time. As his editor, and closest friend, Mark knew he had to dig deeper to find out what the deal was. After the first read, he'd called and tried to get him to talk about it. But he was evasive as usual. And Mark was getting frustrated. He wanted to know all about the latest heroine. Was she real? Was this a composite character? Who was she? What was her real name? How did they meet? But when asked, C.A. said only that "art imitates life." That's it. At the time, Mark had laughed and said he may not want to talk now, but someday it'd all come out. He'd have to come clean. And now he was convinced there was something huge happening with C.A. McLain and he'd find out what it was…one way or another.

######

The book was selling well. A new press release would hit tomorrow, to give it a boost, and C.A. wanted to see it. Usually, he didn't much care. But this time, it was personal. His phone beeped twice, indicating email had arrived, and he quickly grabbed it and scanned the attachment.

"Son of a Bitch!" he swore loudly. His face muscles tightened, his eyes blazed. *No way. No fucking way this could be happening.*

Calling Mark, he waited impatiently, tapping his fingertips on the desk until he answered. One, two, three rings. *Damnit Mark, pick up.* Four, five.

"Mark Simeon, can I…"

He didn't wait for the rest.

"You SOB, what the hell is this?" he roared into the phone.

"Calm down. What's what?"

"You know damn well *what's what!*" he replied. "First in the new Max Colby series? There is no series, damn you. I told you that."

"And I told you this was too good. Readers want more. You agreed, remember?"

"I never agreed and you know it." He was seething now.

"Slow down buddy, listen. You left them hanging."

"Did not."

"Did too."

"How so?"

"Jade."

"Huh?"

"Your heroine, Jade, remember?"

"What about her?" his voice sounded sheepish now.

"She and Max. They didn't get together yet…"

"It was a murder mystery, not a romance."

"Yeah," Mark chuckled, "so you said."

"Mark, I'm not going to do it again."

"Look. Just think about it. We'll talk when you get into town on the 4th."

"I'm not coming."

"Yes, you are. Julie's had this planned for a long time. She'll make my life miserable if you're a no-show."

He sighed. "So who am I this year?"

Mark chuckled, "Same people coming. So you're still a personal chef who loves to travel."

"Fine. I'll see you then." He said with resignation. He'd been raked in again and he knew it. "Tell Jules Hi for me."

"Will do," Mark answered cheerfully, which seemed to annoy him even more.

"And Mark?" He kept his voice deceptively calm.

"Yeah, buddy," Mark replied in the same calm tone.

"You ever pull this again I'm finding another editor."

Mark chuckled. "Yeah, whatever big guy. See you in a few."

Mark hung up and leaned back, his face narrowed in concentration. *Well, one thing*, he thought, *her name isn't really Jade. So we can rule out any Jades in his mysterious past.* He tapped his fingers on the desk. Now, if he could only trick him into revealing her real name. He smiled as the idea formed. "Yeah, that'll work," he whispered to himself. "That will definitely work."

C.A. hung up the phone and stood gazing out the window. From his cabin's study, he could see the wide expanse of the lake, the trees in full leaf for the summer. The breeze blew softly off the water, and the ripples seemed to rhythmically move across the lake. It was beautiful to watch, and a sudden melancholy enveloped him. She should be here, standing next to him. Watching with him. Instead, she was inside him. Inside his heart, as if trapped there forever.

Chapter 4

Annie leaned back and closed her eyes. She felt like her safe little world had been shattered. All she could see in her head was Chris, and she knew that it would be a long time before she could erase that image again. It had taken her 5 long years to erase it the first time. And 5 more years when her world was shattered a second time.

The memories came flooding back. No way to stop them. Especially with half of them right there in black and white. *How could anyone have done this to her?* she thought. It was cruel and devastatingly hurtful. Reliving every embarrassing detail of her ill-fated friendship with Chris.

She'd only been 18 when they met. And from that moment on, for her anyway, it was hook line and sinker. Outwardly they were just friends. Good friends, but platonic. Not once in 7 years did they cross that line, though the undertones were always there. Then, the one time when they might have just taken that step, it all blew up.

She knew she needed to find him. Prove to herself that it couldn't be him. She'd track him down, that's what she'd do. She strode purposefully over to her dresser and yanked open the top drawer. Reaching in the back, she pulled out her old journal. It was as good a place to start as any. His old address was in there somewhere, and she could start with that. She knew he'd moved since then of course, but some of these new people-finding search engines went back pretty far.

She went back out to the living room, grabbed her laptop and powered it up. *Nothing like the internet to hunt someone down*, she thought with a wry smirk.

She started with the college alumni directory. The online directory allowed her to search by name, and she quickly entered Chris Gregory in the search field.

It came up instantly, and Annie sighed with frustration. Nothing. Just his name, degree, and the year he graduated. No current employment information. No address, phone or email. "Damn!" she swore softly. Okay, moving along to the next strategy. Social Media; Facebook. LinkedIn. "Where are you?" Annie said in frustration. *Wait… Instagram*! He was an amateur photographer, he must be there. Nope. Twitter? Trying both his real name and the author's name, she continued googling and even went to other search engines, blogs, etc. Nothing. He's unlisted. This was going to be tough. Or costly. Even the basic directory searches were turning up nothing. Only his old addresses. Nothing current. And cell phone numbers, well forget that. Smacking her forehead, she thought of course she can't find him. He's deliberately made himself unable to be found. It would be a long night, she thought miserably. He'd disappeared from her life, for the second time, 5 years ago, and it looked like it was going to take another 20 to find him. She shut down the laptop, stood and stretched, and headed back to her room. Fleetingly, she wondered if Sam were still in touch with him. No, she wouldn't reach out to Sam. Not again. She'd sleep, wake up and forget the whole thing. She'd never been particularly ambitious or industrious. Giving up was the best option.

######

But Luce wasn't ready to give up so easily and it seems within a week, she'd set up a lunch date with Annie's friend Jen, an editor at one of the biggest publishing houses in New York. She knew Jen might not know the secret life behind the author, but she knew enough about the industry, and the way authors sometimes hide their identities, to help. Plus she was one of the few people Annie trusted. Her sister didn't surround herself with a large social network. She chose her friends carefully, and kept them close.

Annie scanned the crowded dining room at O'Neals. Luce loved "doing lunch" here, mostly because it was packed with brokers, and Luce decided long ago to follow the money. It wasn't that she never dated men who weren't loaded, it was simply that Luce figured she could love a rich guy just as easily as a poor one.

Even though she knew this whole thing was futile, and Jen would probably have a good laugh at the whole idea, Annie agreed to meet with them anyway. What the hell, her life was just turned upside down anyway. She spotted Luce and Jen at a corner table by the window. She let out a small laugh, knowing that Luce tipped dearly for that table. It was the window watching table. You could see the front entrance, and she could ogle all she wanted without being seen. Jen didn't seem to mind the view either. The two sat giggling away like silly teenagers as Annie approached.

The old sibling jealousy reared up momentarily, how Luce used to monopolize Annie's friends and Annie felt left out. *Grow up!* She chastised herself.

Jen looked up first and smiled warmly. "Hey Annie, long time no see!"

Annie smiled back. "I know! You with your busy skyrocketing career and all!"

Luce looked up and grinned.

"Hey sis! You look smashing today."

Annie knew Luce was just being sarcastic. She didn't approve of anything Annie picked out herself. So Annie did what any self-respecting woman would do and stuck her tongue out and made a face.

"Oh very mature, sis. Sit. What are you gonna eat?"

A small smile played on her lips, as she pretended to think about it.

After a brief moment, she smiled broadly.

"Molten Lava Cake," Annie announced.

Luce glared at Annie.

"You will not have dessert for lunch. Try the salmon, it's delicious. And you don't need all those calories anyway!"

"Nope, dessert it is. I'm neurotic and depressed right now, and I have to feed my soul. What's a few more pounds anyway?" she sighed. Luce had always been the thin, svelte one. Annie had always been the slightly chubby one. Some things would never change.

Jen laughed out loud knowing this was nothing more than sibling bickering. "You guys are *so* entertaining, and we *definitely* have to do this more often."

Annie glanced over at New York's hottest rising publishing star. Jen was one of those warm and friendly women you can't help liking instantly. She was outgoing, and like Annie, had no pretenses. She wasn't a size zero, she typically had her thick wavy brown hair swept up haphazardly in a clip, and shopped at vintage retro thrift stores instead of Neiman Marcus. Which is exactly where Annie had met her just a few years earlier. She was so damn nice they became fast friends. Jen had a spontaneity and a spark that Annie couldn't resist. It was the ying to her yang. The fact that Jen had married a man she'd known only 3 weeks had Annie both jealous and in awe all at the same time. To her it was the most romantic story ever. Slightly awkward bookworm meets handsome southern cabbie, the horse drawn kind, and rides around the park all night with him. They fly off to Vegas and get married after dinner one night. They bought a little house in Queens, had 2 children, and he still brings her flowers home at least once a week.

And where was Annie's handsome cabbie? Annie sighed, drawing a look from both her lunch companions.

"What gives Annie? Why the long face?"

She looked pointedly at Jen. "Just thinking…why can't I meet a fabulous guy at the park and run away with him weeks later and live happily ever after? Do you realize how lucky you are?"

"I know, it was right out of book, I tell you," Jen laughed as she covered one of Annie's hands with her own. "And now it looks like it's your turn!"

Looking over at Luce, she smiled. "And then it will be yours!"

"Sorry, Jen, I'm not the romantic type. I like my diamonds polished, thank you"

"You're such a bitch, Luce," Jen smiled wryly.

"Yeah, same to you, Jen" Luce laughed.

"So," Jen turned to Annie and smiled. "Luce thinks you might be the muse? I can't believe you didn't call me, like the first instant you realized it!"

"Luce also thinks that a man's worth is in his wallet, doesn't make her right. And I would have called but you told me you were inundated this week and wouldn't be coming up for air, remember?" Annie knew she was bending the truth, but didn't want Jen to feel left out.

"Well, notwithstanding Luce's dementia, the character Jade, and my workload, why do you think McLain's book is about you?" Jen was genuinely curious. Ever since McLain's new book had hit the proverbial shelves rumors were rampant about it. Everyone was talking. Jen knew it could be just marketing buzz but it felt too real to be a sales ruse.

"I don't anymore. It was just my imagination gone haywire." Annie grabbed a menu pretending to study it.

"You know Annie, always the great pretender," Luce interjected.

"Cork it Luce, let Annie talk," replied Jen with a laugh.

Annie looked up over at Jen. "What's to say, Jen, this was Luce's cockeyed plan, not mine. At first, I read the book and got a little weirded out because some of the scenes were so real in my head. Things that had happened to me. At least I think they did. Memory's a funny thing, ya know? Anyway, then as I read more, it got worse, because it's as if he'd gotten right into my head and pulled my thoughts out and written them for the world to see. But, after careful consideration," Annie paused for effect. "After very very careful consideration, I realized that he could have been writing about anyone. Most women experience these situations in their lives once or twice. Most women have these feelings at least once or twice, or in my case hundreds of times. You see my point?"

"Wasn't there anything in the book that didn't fit? Something that doesn't apply?"

"No, nada, zippo, zilch. You know the one part where she gets dumped in college by a total jerk? And he takes her to a local dive bar to get drunk and let off steam? Or when she told him how afraid she was to change majors so he went with her. Waited outside while she talked to the dean, took her out to celebrate?"

"Wait!" Annie suddenly jumped up from her chair and laid her palms on the table. "That's it! Max is carrying this grudge because Rick tells him that Jade is in love with Rick and to just forget about her!" Annie was on a roll. "Not what happened to me, I mean yeah, Sam once asked me if I had a thing for Chris. But I told him flat out that I did. So unless Sam lied through his teeth, which I sincerely doubt, that triangle thing was all news to me! And what happened to us next of course is completely left out of the book."

Annie sat back down breathless but triumphant.

Jen shook her head, laughing. "Hold up. Chris, he's the guy you think is supposed to be Max Colby?"

"No, I don't. Luce does."

"OK, and Sam is his best friend, who in the book, is Rick?"

"Yep."

"I did manage to read it by the way and you're right. Rick tells Max that Jade's in love with Rick and it crushed him."

"I think my head is spinning" complained Luce, laughing.

"Annie go on. In real life, what happened when you told Sam you were in love with Chris?"

"First off, I didn't quite say I was in love with him. I think I just said I was maybe interested in him, as more than friends? I mean I was head over heels, but I wasn't going to tell anyone that. Anyway, if Sam told Chris about it, which I'm sure he did, it certainly didn't *crush* him. In fact, that's when Chris disappeared from my life. And I don't mean he just pulled back from me like I had the plague. Nope, took off without me on the adventure of a lifetime that WE were supposed to have together. It broke my heart. I always regretted telling Sam how I felt. I didn't know if he'd tell Chris, though I probably secretly wanted him to, because I honestly thought Chris had some feelings for me. I never imagined he'd ditch me." Annie's voice was breaking, and her eyes were tearing. She grabbed a napkin and dabbed at them. Trying to stop the impending waterfall. "And that most definitely isn't in the book."

Jen took her hand and squeezed it gently. "Take a deep breath Annie, and relax." Annie complied, and felt herself gaining control.

Jen continued. "Tell me more. An adventure?"

Annie sighed and shrugged her shoulders. "So Chris submitted these photos he took for a photo contest and they were so amazing he not only won, but they offered him a gig. In Ireland! I was totally amazed and excited for him, but utterly depressed at the thought of him being gone for so long. Months maybe. I as much as told him so, well not so much. But I did say I wanted to go with him and he said OK, and my whole world just lit up, Jen. I mean ask Luce, I was on top of the world. Until he left without me. Just kaboom. No note, no phone call. Just kaboom."

Somehow saying it that way softened the rush of sadness that took over whenever she thought about it. She had been all packed, ready to go. He'd pick her up in the morning on the way to the airport. Only he didn't show. She waited downstairs in front of the duplex she'd been sharing with a few other recent grads, until she knew beyond a doubt it was too late to catch their flight. She knew he wasn't coming. Oh at first she thought the worst had happened. An accident maybe… somehow he couldn't reach her. It had to be something disastrous. Until Sam called her. All he said was that Chris had left and not to wait for him any longer. No other explanation. She called Sam back a few times to get more info, but he just clammed up. Said she'd be better off moving on. "Forget it," he said. Like that would ever ever happen.

"Wait, this was after you told Sam how you felt about Chris? Even if Chris didn't return your feelings, he obviously cared about you, this doesn't make sense."

"Oh really Jen, are you that naive?" Luce interrupted. "If he wasn't in love with her it would make perfect sense. He'd want to avoid encouraging her. Which is what I told her back then. On that very long drive home since you know it was me that had to help her move back."

"Or, maybe Sam didn't tell him what you said. Maybe he lied." Jen spoke abruptly. "Think about it. In the book, Max is told the love of his life is in love with his best friend. So maybe that's what really happened, and Chris backed off because he was hurt. Couldn't face being just friends."

"Backed off? Oh that's a nice way to put it. But still, wouldn't that have been a kicker," Annie said longingly.

"This is interesting, I gotta tell you." Jen was getting pretty jazzed up. "Think about it. If Sam lied to Chris, and Chris is C.A., then maybe, just maybe, he's written what he wants to have been the truth. He has Jade lie about her feelings to Rick, because he wishes that you lied to Sam…and deep down you loved him but wouldn't admit it."

Jen stopped talking to let it all sink in.

"Annie, this guy is one of the most reclusive, elusive authors around. Ask Luce! Getting anywhere near him is all but impossible. I'm guessing it was a marketing ploy with his first novel, and since then they've had to keep up the mystery. Every author needs a hook you know. With the exception of probably his publishing house, and maybe only one or two people there no one knows who C.A. McLain really is. And believe me, a lot of effort's been made by a whole lot of people to find out."

"Trust me, I know, I'm one of them," Annie shook her head and laughed.

"Well, then, thankfully my friend, you have me."

"What does that mean, Jen?" Annie looked at her friend curiously. "What are you up to?"

"So, I didn't want to say anything until I'd heard your version of things, we all know how Luce tends to spin everything… but now that I have? You know how every year you beg me to come to the park for the 4th of July concert? And every year I tell you I can't, it's a work thing?"

"Oh! You're going to come this year? And how exactly is this helping my cause?"

"No, still a work thing. But it's the exact nature of the work thing. It's a party at the Simeons. I've got an invite."

"Not following Jen. Who are the Simeons?"

"Mark Simeon. Taylor Publishing? Editor for the one and only C.A. McLain? Is this ringing a bell folks?"

Annie sat stunned, her mouth hanging open, her drink tipping precariously as she digested this. "How the hell would I know who edits this guy's books, Jen, I mean really!"

"Who cares," Luce jumped in. "That's too perfect."

"I'm going to bring you as my date Annie," Jen giggled a bit as she said it.

"You want me to crash a party?"

"Don't be silly, usually Bill goes with me to these things, we'll just swap you for Bill. I'm sure they won't mind. I've worked with Mark on a few projects now, even met his wife a few times. If it eases your mind, I'll check with them first."

"I don't know Jen. Maybe this isn't such a good idea."

"What's the worst that can happen?" Jen asked.

"Oh I don't know, he's there and doesn't want to see me? Or it's not him, it's a complete stranger writing about someone else? It would be mortifying."

Luce shook her head in mock despair.

"You are just hopeless Annie. Of course if it's him he'll want to see you. Even I can figure that out."

Jen grinned. "And the best thing that can happen? You reunite. Recap. He loved you Annie. He was going to whisk you off to Ireland for god's sake. But then he learns you loved Sam. He's devastated. He goes off alone, and at some point, he begins writing. And now, years later, he writes THE novel of his life," Jen was really playing it up now. "Calling out to our very own Annie here. And we need to make sure you answer."

Luce nodded, but her expression clearly indicated she wasn't fully on board. Her first priority was keeping Annie from being hurt.

Jen paused and leaned back as their server arrived with their food.

Jen continued her inquisition as she took a small bite of her salad. "Tell me about Chris. I cannot believe you've never mentioned him. No wonder you won't let me fix you up, you're probably still fixated on him! Describe him as best you can physically. Who knows, maybe he's attended a writer's conference or two, incognito, maybe a workshop. There's always speculation. Whispered rumors that he's in the back row. You know how people are."

"Chris isn't C.A." Annie took a large bite of her cake and grinned sheepishly as the liquid chocolate center dripped on her shirt. Luce frowned, reaching out to wipe it off as Annie batted her hand away and laughed.

"How do you know that?" asked Jen. "Luce said you have a whole list. Shouldn't we eliminate the obvious first? Just tell me what he looks like."

Annie blushed. "Hmmm. Let's see. Tall, hunky, the kind of guy you just want to grab and, well you know," Annie's voice suddenly seemed lower. More sensual.

Annie tipped her head slightly, and closed her eyes, picturing him.

"Those eyes. Oh my those eyes. Blue as the Caribbean. Short, wavy golden brown hair. Tall, maybe 6 feet, taller possibly at my height it's all the same. Lean but built, ooooooooh don't make me do this!" Annie whined suddenly. "I can't. I can't just sit here and picture him." Annie sighed wistfully. "He was beautiful. Inside and out. And oh so sweet." Annie's voice trailed off.

She looked over at Jen, who suddenly had a very odd expression on her face.

"Sharp pointy nose?" she asked.

"Oh, no. Broad, distinguished."

"And the chin?"

"Definite cleft. Very chiseled. High cheek bones too, by the way."

"Wow. Just wow." Jen sat up very straight in her chair a look of determination on her face.

"What?" Annie and Luce both shouted at once.

"That's a perfect description of a guy I met last year at the American Author's Symposium. Real quiet, laid back guy. Didn't talk to many people. Just seemed to roam around most of the time, watching everyone else. Didn't participate much. I only noticed him because he stood in front of me at the breakfast buffet. And he was *very* attractive" Jen winked and grinned. "Yes, very attractive."

"Jen, you're a married woman for christ's sake," Luce shook her head laughing.

"Married, Luce, not dead. Anyway, I introduced myself, but he never did tell me his name. I remember he kind of brushed over that. Just shook my hand and said he was pleased to meet me. I thought it was weird. Ended up sitting down and eating together, chatting for a good long while actually. When was the last time you saw him?"

"Right after I got engaged" Annie whispered, the memory haunting her even now.

"O. M. G., you were married?" This was news to Jen. "Okay, *this* you never told me."

"Because I wasn't. I didn't go through with it, and it's before I met you, but that's a whole other story."

"Right, ok. You and I are sooo having a girl's weekend soon. Anyway, tell me about your last conversation with Chris."

"How much time do you have?" Annie almost smiled as she asked.

"Long story?"

"Long, long sad tale, yes," Annie replied.

"Give me the short version then." Jen was not going to be deterred.

"OK. Short short version. A few years after Chris took off and deserted me," Annie paused for effect, "I met Larry. Good looking. Guy-next-door type I guess. Not too ambitious but great sense of humor. We hit it off. Dated for a while. He got a job offer in Florida, and proposed. I said yes. So wedding plans are in motion, and my life is completely spinning out of control and one night there's a knock at the door. I open it. And there's Chris."

"Holy shit," Jen said, almost involuntarily. "Sorry, go on."

"At first I just stared. I did not say a single thing. Then I just kind of waved him in."

"It was totally awkward at first. He sat down on the couch. I got him a beer. He asked how I'd been, la la la… small talk. I asked him what he was doing, and he just kind of said this and that. I was completely floored mind you. I mean I hadn't been in touch with him in 5 years. So I asked him, 'how did you find me?' and he said alumni directory. I figured ok, probably legit. Then I went for the jugular. I said, and I remember this clearly, I said 'Chris,

45

why the hell did you take off without me?' and he just looked at me with this odd expression and said 'Wasn't it obvious?' and I said 'Noooo, explain it.' Needless to say he did not explain. Just said it was all in the note. I got mad. He got mad. He noticed the ring on my finger. Stared at my hand, stared at me. Being mad, I took full advantage of the moment to grab an invitation from the box on the table, and hand it to him. He looks at it, reads it, then he asked if he could bring a date, his girlfriend. I said I didn't care if he brought godzilla. There was lots more, but like I said, it didn't go well. It ended with him storming out. We haven't spoken since. I know it's seems absurd, here I was engaged, but I was so ticked off that he just waltzes back into my life. Telling me about a girlfriend no less. I mean looking back, it's ridiculous. But as long as he was unattached I had a chance."

"But you were engaged, Annie, so why did you care?"

"I suppose I knew deep down it was wrong. The relationship I mean. I was hoping Chris would be jealous. Guess the joke was on me."

"Guess it was," Luce shot back. "I liked Larry, by the way, he was a nice guy. At least I thought he was. Guess you never can tell, though."

Annie brushed the hair out of her eyes in a flustered gesture.

"This is too amazing," Jen continued, her voice picking up momentum. "Listen. I told you we had breakfast together. I had asked this guy if he'd brought his wife, and he said he wasn't married. And he got this very sad look in his eyes. Almost empty. So I asked him what happened? You know me, can't keep my mouth shut. But he didn't seem to care. I don't even know if he heard me. He just launched into this sad tale. He told me about the girl who got away. I don't know why he told me. Funny I'd forgotten all about that though at the time it definitely struck me. I don't remember all the details, but it definitely was a very very similar tale. There was one thing though, kind of stuck out. Annie what's your dream home? If you could live anywhere in any kind of home?"

"That's easy," laughed Luce. "Little house with a white picket fence, right Annie?"

Annie smiled. "Yeah. Sorry. That's it for me though. Especially if it's on the ocean. Like on Cape Cod, or the east end of Long Island. Maybe Fire Island."

Jen smiled. "One thing I do remember, he told me she's probably living in her little white house with the white picket fence in Nantucket with some jerk who doesn't deserve her."

They all sat in silence allowing that to sink in.

"Chris knew about your dream house?" Luce spoke first, a little miffed. "I thought I was the only one you told."

"He's the only other person I've told. Well, except mom. And Steve, the gardener across the street. Might of told the mailman. Anyway, Chris and I spent all night once studying for exams. And we started imagining our perfect home. He wanted an old stone manor and I wanted small and simple."

"Oh my god!" The words tumbled out of Annie's mouth. "Oh my god the stone manor. In the book. Oh my god!" She stood up, then sat down.

Then stood up again. At which point Luce and Jen grabbed her and sat her down.

"Annie, pay attention. Did Chris send you a wedding gift?" Jen asked.

Annie thought for a moment. "No, I don't think so. But then again, I didn't look at most of them. Luce dealt with it for me. It was kind of a bad break up."

"You can say that again," Luce remarked caustically. "She dumped him a week before the wedding, and made me and our mom deal with returning gifts and calling the guests."

"I said I was sorry, but you know I was a wreck."

"This guy said something about his gift being returned," Jen spoke up. "This has got to be your guy. Question, if you didn't really love Larry, what made it so hard?"

"He cheated on me." Annie replied with a shrug. It had been 5 years, and she'd known then that it was actually for the best. But nobody likes to be played a fool!

"Oh well that sucks, definitely dump worthy. Was it like a one-night stand or did he have someone on the side?"

"One-night stand."

"Nympho Nora strikes again," Luce piped in.

"Nympho Nora?" Now Jen was really intrigued. "I'm gonna need to start a list of questions for that girls' weekend."

"All right, girls, time for a plan." Jen beamed, as if this whole thing had made her day. She'd been so buried in her work lately, she could use a little adventure with friends!

"Look, guys, I appreciate this but you both ought to know better than to encourage this little fantasy of mine. I have plenty already. You'll end up pushing me over the edge and right into the loony bin."

Luce and Jen glanced at each other, and smiled. Turning to Annie, they both spoke simultaneously.

"Let's do it!" their voices were mischievous, and Annie took a deep breath and sighed. This was trouble with a capital T.

Chapter 5

Annie read the group text message from Jen the next day and sighed.

Jen: *My house. Thursday. 7.*

She quickly texted back.

Thought we'd been over this. Stupid idea.

She glanced down when her phone buzzed.

Luce: *It's on. I'll drive. End of discussion.*

Annie sighed. This whole business was getting out of hand. Maybe McLain was Chris. Maybe he wasn't. And even if he was, that doesn't mean she's Jade. Even if she is Jade, it doesn't make it true. It doesn't mean those feelings that he wrote in the book were his. And if they weren't, she'd feel even more idiotic than she already did. Her head was spinning from all these thoughts and a few weeks at a nice rest home were starting to sound real tempting. When her phone buzzed again, she reached for it automatically, ready to fire off another quick barb, only it wasn't Jen or Luce.

Back Off.

Whoa. OK, what the hell? Must be a wrong number. Not gonna reply, she thought. Happens all the time. She swiped to delete the message and went back to obsessing over the book. And Chris.

When she and Luce arrived at Jen's on Thursday, they had to circle the block 5 times before they found a parking space. Typical. In Queens, they had this nutty alternate side of the street parking rule. Some days you parked on one side, then you had to move your car to the other side for alternate days. It was nuts. But the bottom line was there was only one side of the street available for parking, and circling was about the only way to get a spot. It was all the way at the other end of the block, and by the time they reached Jen's, Annie regretted her choice of shoes. They were new, and pinched her toes. She much preferred her worn out canvas slip-ons, but Luce kept making faces at her and calling her names, goading her till she broke down and bought these stupid things. *Note to self* she thought, *do not shoe shop with Luce ever again.*

When Jen opened the front door, she was greeted with a scowl by Annie, while Luce stood next to her looking a little too smug.

"OK. What happened now? Come on in, take your shoes off and tell me."

"Bless you Jen!" cried Annie with delight as she sped inside the foyer and slipped the horrible things off her feet. Wriggling her toes, she did a little dance and turned around and beamed at Jen. "You are the best hostess in the world, did anyone ever tell you that?"

"Let's just say you're not the first!" Jen laughed as she turned to Luce. "How bout you? No niceties for the hostess?"

Luce laughed out loud. "Jen, my sister is the biggest crybaby in the world. Can't even wear a decent pair of shoes for one night. Like it would kill her to look, or act, like a grown woman for once."

"I for one don't see that it's all it's cracked up to be, Luce!" Jen laughed as she showed them into the small, cozy living room.

"Well, if it isn't my favorite sisters! I hear we've got a mystery going on!" the voice boomed through the house, startling the two women. But the look on their faces was pure delight when Jen's husband Bill entered. He was, by any standard, an amazing specimen. He was huge, in a lumberjack sort of way, with a shaggy mop of flaming red hair, a big open smile and bright green eyes. The kind of guy you couldn't help liking immediately.

"Bill is a little too excited about all this" Jen winked up at Bill as she spoke. 11 years and she still absolutely delighted in him. She adored him, and it was evident from the look on her face.

As Luce stood up to say hello he drew her into a bear hug, and laughed as he let go of her and swiveled around to grab Annie. Annie was about a third of his size, but always enjoyed the experience nonetheless. Being held in a bear hug by a big friendly guy like Bill was actually kind of exhilarating.

"What's your pleasure, ladies?" drawled Bill. "I was told it was daiquiri night, I suppose since I'm real good at those. Fresh frozen by the way, just pick a flavor. Banana, Strawberry, or Piña Colada if you're really nice," he chuckled to himself.

"Piña Colada!" Luce and Annie both called out in unison.

"You got it. Just hang tight and I'll have them to you in a jif." He swung back around and suddenly looked very serious. His eyes narrowed. "Don't you girls start talking till I get back, ya hear? I don't want to miss any of this. I've got my two cents to put in ya know!" Then he smiled broadly and headed into the kitchen.

"Sorry, but when I told Bill about the book, he got all excited and he really really wants to help, you don't mind do you?" Jen's voice was almost apologetic.

"The more the merrier," murmured Annie grudgingly.

"Don't worry Jen, not a problem!" Luce seemed a little more easygoing about it. Of course, thought Annie, it's not her damn problem.

When Bill returned with the drinks, and a spare pitcher for refills, Jen decided to get started.

"OK, ladies, let's get this show on the road."

Luce and Annie just looked at her.

"Details. I need details. Since we're going to this shindig on the 4th, I thought maybe the more you could tell me about your Chris, the better equipped I'll be. You can bet that if he's there he won't be going as C.A. McLain. Too many guests. I'll need to be on the lookout."

"You think he'll be there Jen?" Annie whispered. Almost afraid of the answer. "Of course you do. Of course he will."

"I need to know more Annie so I can spot him before he spots you. So you can maintain control. No room for error here."

"Well, I don't know what more I can tell you Jen, I mean, it's been a long time."

"Excuse me ladies," Bill interjected. "Annie, I hate to sound like a big ol' dumb redneck here, but do you have a picture maybe? Online? Anything?"

"Funny you should ask, Bill. And I think it's a very intelligent question." Annie flashed a smile at Bill, and setting her drink down, reached into her purse.

Luce and Jen both glared at Annie. "Sis, you had a damn picture and didn't show me?"

"Yeah, Annie, what's up with that?" Jen was miffed too.

Annie shrugged them off.

Gently pulling the photo from her purse, she laid it on her lap and gently smoothed her palm over it, as if to make sure it wouldn't crease, or worse, wipe off. She'd kept the photo for years. Tucked away, hidden in a drawer. Never showed a soul. She didn't know why she'd placed it in her purse today, just figured it was time to bring him back out.

Resting her hands over the photo, she looked down and paused for a long moment. Finally, raising her head up, she lifted the photo and passed it to Jen gingerly.

"Please," she whispered. "Be careful. It's my only one, k?" She'd scanned it of course. Stashed in the cloud forever. But there was just something about having the original.

Jen gave Annie a reassuring look.

"Don't worry. It's safe."

She looked down at the photo and studied it hard. Her eyes creased as she tipped it at an angle, as if to get a better look. The photo was over a decade old and the colors had faded just a little. But it was clear as mud.

Handing it back, she looked directly at Annie.

"That's him. The guy I met in Florida."

"You met a guy in Florida?" Bill feigned shock. "Why is the husband always the last to know?" he exclaimed with a laugh.

"Excuse me, do I get to see?" Luce was annoyed. All this time Annie had been holding out on her.

Without so much as glancing at Luce, Annie reached out and handed her the photo. Staring at Jen, her eyes wide, she began gnawing on her lip. Her stomach began flip flopping and she took a deep breath to relax. Then another. Not working.

"Ok," she let out the breath she'd been holding. "So. So, he is a writer. But Jen, it doesn't mean it's him." Annie's protest came out sounding weak.

"No, it doesn't. But, if he's at the party, there's kind of a hundred percent chance it is. And the only way we'll know is if we go."

"No, Jen. I don't think I can do it." Annie's voice was quavering. "You go and report back. I mean what if he's there and he's not, you know, alone? What if he's there with some hot model or actress. Or worse he's there, he's alone, but doesn't say two words to me."

"Can I say something here please?" Bill interjected. "I do know something about this you know, being a guy. In fact I'm a guy that read the book. And from where I sit, Annie, he's definitely writing about someone real in his life. Secondly, he's obviously head over heels with her. He writes about her with, oh, I don't know, a reverence that's beautiful. I wish I could tell Jen how I felt that way. I don't have the words like your man here does, but I sure know what he's feeling."

"But see, Bill, that's the problem. Maybe it's Chris. And maybe he used this whole thing to write a good book. Maybe he had those feelings for someone else and put me in there cause he's afraid to reveal the truth." Annie sounded desolate, and somewhat desperate, and Bill shot her a sympathetic look.

"Annie, that's the whole point of the book." Bill's voice was softer now, gentler. "I got it, didn't you? He took a chance, and now he wants his Jade, or maybe it's Annie, to do the same. You have to go for it. At least find out the truth. You owe yourself that much. You owe him that much too."

"What's the plan Jen? Give it up, let's see if you're as crafty as you think," Luce was all in now.

Little miss enthusiasm, thought Annie. She wouldn't be so cocky if she were the one in this situation. Annie sighed. Luce would never be in this situation. When Luce wants something, or someone, she goes for it. She's not a wimp. *Hey wait!* Annie thought, *I'm no wimp*! She knew with sudden clarity what she needed to do. She straightened up, determined.

"I'm in!" Annie suddenly spoke. "If it's not him, no harm done. If it is and it all goes south, so what. Haven't seen him in five years, won't see him for another twenty."

"Good for you Annie," Jen beamed at her new protégé, "it's all gonna be perfect, you'll see. We'll go, and scope it out. If he's there, I'll be by your side to prop you up. And I'll find out the deal with this book. If I can't get anything out of him, I'll go to Mark and fess up. This will all work out in the end, one way or another. That much I promise. Just one more thing. What's Chris's last name?"

"Gregory," Annie replied with a little sigh, nervously gnawing on her lower lip now. Maybe this is a hugely bad idea. How she could go from being confident and ready to simply ready for disaster?

Shaking off the anxiety, Annie somehow managed to relax after that, probably the second, or third Piña Colada took care of that. And they all enjoyed dinner and dessert with no further mention of Chris Gregory, aka C.A. McLain. Maybe.

######

Annie paced across her bedroom floor, chewing on her fingernails, stopping every so often to listen, maybe the phone was ringing. "Damn it, call already," she said out loud. "OK, then text. TEXT ME!" She stared at her phone. Jen had to have spoken to Mark by now. She'd promised to call the minute she'd cleared it for her to go to the party. This is ridiculous, she thought. Her stomach was doing flips, and she placed a hand over her belly to qualm it. She was crazy to even contemplate doing this. But there was really no turning back.

Plopping down on her king size bed, which she'd bought with her first real paychecks, and had taken 3 years to pay off, she laid down with her hands behind her head and stared at the ceiling. "Ok, Google, play Drops of Jupiter," Annie called out. Time for one last trip down memory lane with the song that played the night they met. And sadly seemed to forever be 'their song.'

Suddenly it hit her. What a monstrously bad idea this all was. A wave of melancholy moved through her like a tsunami. Where was Chris right now? she wondered. Would he really be at that party? *Damn*, Annie thought, *I should go incognito. Hide in the bushes maybe look for him. No, better yet, I'll walk right in and spot him immediately. He'll turn and see me. Our eyes will lock. He'll come rushing over and throw his arms around me and kiss me, ooooooh, it will be so fine.* She sighed and closed her eyes, willing her body to relax.

That's it! She sat up, running her fingers through her hair. That's the whole problem. We never actually kissed. Hugged, yeah, held hands, sure, but never actually kissed. *I'm stuck in a time warp of lost love because I never found out what came next.* It finally dawned on her that it's not having the experience. Maybe, just maybe he's a lousy kisser, worse even than Mickey in Florida all those years ago. She shuddered just thinking about it. And maybe if we had dated we'd have ended up apart anyway. Maybe all those butterflies in my stomach would have eventually disappeared. It's the not knowing that's doing this. If I could just find out I could be done with it. Startled at her own self-realization, she suddenly felt calmer than she had in years. I'm still in love with the unknown and that's all it is. He's probably balding, out of shape, and been married 7 times already. To younger women who just want his money. Maybe Jen met a guy who just *looked* like Chris did years ago. Maybe.

Feeling only slightly better now, Annie decided she didn't need to wait for Jen's call. She didn't need to go to the party. She didn't need to dwell on it anymore. She'd just go to sleep, and when she woke up in the morning, she'd be ready to move on. The case of the lost love over.

She hadn't been asleep more than a few minutes when the ringing started. Disoriented, she reached out to get the phone and smacked into the lamp with her hand. Fumbling around on the nightstand, she located her phone and picked it up.

"What, yeah, I mean… hello?"

"Sorry Annie, you must have been sleeping, eh, it's Jen, so wake up!"

"Jen," Annie said sleepily, "what's up?" Annie was unusually calm.

"Annie, it's me Jen. Wake up. The party is a go."

Annie stomach flipped. *Stay strong*, she thought.

"Wow, um, ok, but Jen, I have to tell you, I've had an epiphany."

"Oh do tell!" Jen laughed. She knew somehow Annie was going to try and back out.

"Sure. OK. I realized that the only reason I'm still pining away for Chris is because we never went out. Never had hot steamy sex. Never so much as kissed. I figured it out. It's the not knowing. I realized that if we had, I wouldn't be wishing for it. I'd have already had it. So, no more pining. I'm going out and starting my life. "

"Too bad."

"What do you mean, too bad? Jen, you're supposed to say, 'atta girl Annie. You go for it.' Not 'too bad.'"

"Too bad."

"OK." Annie sighed. "I give. Why too bad? No wait, I know. I know. He's going to be there, isn't he." It wasn't really a question anymore. Even in her twilight state at the moment she knew deep down this was all going to blow up.

Jen spoke at high speed, the words pouring out so fast she didn't catch her breath once.

"Yes, he is. Listen, I can be very clever at getting info when I need it. I just asked Mark who was coming this year, you know, anyone interesting, blah blah blah, and he said 'the usual'. And I might have asked about single guys, you know because I was bringing a friend and all…"

Annie groaned. "Really?"

"Really, and lo and behold, are you ready for this? He's got this friend, Chris, probably the only single guy coming. Oh, that's Billie Jr raising a ruckus, I've gotta run!"

"Jen wait!" Annie shouted into the phone. "Did he say what his last name was?"

"Sorry Annie, no time, gotta run. Call you tomorrow."

Annie heard the click and slammed the phone down. *Shit shit shit.* Now her epiphany was over. Kaput. He was going to be there. She knew it deep down in her bones. I'll never sleep tonight she thought. This is absurd.

She closed her eyes and pictured him as best she could. And a small tear escaped to run down her cheek. It wasn't an epiphany after all. It was just an excuse for her behavior. Her life was a washout. And she wasn't the same girl he knew before. Even if she did get to see him, he'd be disappointed. He wouldn't be attracted to her now. If he ever was. Damn, life sucked sometimes.

Jen turned away from the phone and grinned at Bill. "She's trying to back out. I needed to goad her a bit."

"I'd say it sure sounded like goading to me. Hope it works. I really want to see Annie get what she wants. I just hope he's worth it."

Chapter 6

The 4th of July was, by any New Yorker's standards, a perfect day. Low humidity, plenty of sun and clear blue skies. Everyone was making the great escape from the city. The Long Island Expressway was packed, bumper to bumper. If you weren't on the road by 5am, you were going to have an awfully long drive. C.A. hated driving in New York. He hated New York period. So he'd decided to make the trip by train. His hotel was only a few blocks from Penn Station, and the LIRR ran trains to Port Newton virtually all day. He could grab a ride from the station in Port to take him out to Mark's home in North Bay. He hated the trip out there, but he sure loved Mark and Julie's place. It was a smaller home, compared to the surrounding estates. A few wooded acres right on the beach. The small inlet of the LI sound was like a haven to him. The charming old lighthouse rose above the waters at the midpoint between the shores of LI and the Connecticut coastline.

Mark's home sat atop a small hill, the backyard sloping down to the beach. The lawn out back was spattered with children's play equipment, lawn chairs, and miscellaneous toys that posed a hazard to any unsuspecting guests walking barefoot. He smiled as they pulled up in front, already feeling more relaxed. Mark's daughter, Sally, was out front doing her best to greet new arrivals, and at five years old she was already developing a sense of charm that was sure to make anyone feel at home. He had a special affection for Sally, not just because she was his goddaughter, though maybe that was part of it. Sally had a way about her. Her toothless grin seemed to melt him on the spot. And as he stepped out of the car, he immediately knelt down and held out his arms. "Come 'ere, sport," he laughed as he engulfed the small girl in his arms and stood to swing her high in the air. Giggling, she gave him a big wet kiss on the cheek. "Hey big guy! I missed you! You haven't been here in so soooo long!" She swung her mop of blond curls and grinned.

"I missed you too sport. What say you and I go find your dad, then we can go out and have ourselves a swim."

"Okey dokey artichokey!" Sally giggled again and jumping out of his arms, grabbed his hand and started pulling him along.

"Hold up, I need to get my things" he said laughing. Her utter joy was contagious, and he never got tired of it. He may not enjoy these annual summertime rituals, like the big barbecue Julie put on every year, but he sure enjoyed being with this close-knit family. It grounded him, and gave him a sense of normalcy he desperately needed. Ever since his first book hit the bestseller list, life had been a kind of twilight zone. This latest book was another smash. Hit the bestseller list with a bang thanks to the prerelease orders. Even though most of the critics missed the point he'd given them what they craved in a tight suspenseful mystery. Thankfully none of them saw the underlying love story he'd woven in. They called it a touch of romance beneath the dark surface. Hell, what did they know. But he didn't write it for them. He'd written this one for himself. He'd poured his soul into this one and finally exorcised his demons. At least that's what he hoped. For the first time he'd written a book purely for himself, not to entertain or be hailed by the public.

Although in truth, he'd never written for the fame or money. He'd always had a need to tell a story. The celebrity factor had somehow injected itself into his life and he often felt strangled by it. He didn't resent it though, because it afforded him more than he'd hoped. The money was good, especially with the sale of the movie rights. He'd been able to put his younger brothers through college and pay off his parents' mortgage. Not to mention his cabin. That was worth all of it.

He hurried to follow Sally into the house, and moved quickly behind her as she raced right out the back door to the patio. He paused at the door momentarily, and sighed. There must be over 50 people. Most of whom he'd met over the last few years, he guessed. So with a small smile and brief shrug of his shoulders, he ventured outside to make the rounds. For today, he was someone else. Nobody knew who C.A. McLain was. Not even C.A. half the time. Today though, he was just a chef. And he got to use his own name. What a novelty.

He saw Julie first, her long blond hair neatly pulled back in a French braid, her small, slender figure awkwardly trying to balance an enormous tray of hors d'oeuvres as she wormed her way through the cluster of people gathered around the brick patio.

He strode over silently, and smoothly slid the tray from her hands, planting a kiss on her cheek as he did so.

"How's my favorite girl?"

"Much better now that my knight in shining armor has arrived!" Julie looked up at her favorite houseguest, her blue eyes flashing with humor. She genuinely enjoyed having him around, and he knew it. Her affection was honest, and hard to come by. Julie was Mark's high school sweetheart, and though they'd parted for a few years after graduation, they'd both returned home after college, and eventually ended up back together. When Mark began working with him on his first book, he'd spent a lot of weekends here, and Julie had treated him like family from the start. He would do anything for her, and she knew it. Which was why he always dutifully showed up at her annual barbecue. He had no choice, and he accepted that.

And in all the years they'd worked together, Mark had never once let his identity out. He was trustworthy, and would never risk damaging their friendship. Or his livelihood. But it always made him nervous to attend parties like this. If it happened, he'd deal with it. For now he'd put it out of his mind and just try to enjoy himself.

Jen and Annie were the last to arrive. They got a late start, between Jen trying to get Bill and the kids taken care of before leaving and Annie having talked herself in and out of going 50 times. What should have only taken 35 minutes, ended up taking well over 2 hours. Bumper to Bumper traffic and nobody to blame but themselves, so the party was in full swing when they arrived.

Stepping into the main entryway, Annie looked around and sighed.

"You know Jen, I always wanted a house just like this."

"And so you shall have one!" Jen responded with a smile. As excited as Jen was about reigniting this doomed romance of Annie's, she truly wanted happiness for her. And if Chris Gregory was her happiness, Jen was going to see that she gets him. Though she suspected Annie's happiness didn't rely on getting Chris back. But that was for Annie to figure out.

Stepping out to the patio out back, Jen spotted Mark.

"Ok, shh, there's Mark." Jen waved and started in his direction, tugging Annie's arm to drag her along.

They headed over to the barbecue, where Mark stood manning the flames while Julie hovered over making sure nothing burned.

"Hey Jen, good to see you." Mark's greeting was warm and friendly, and left no doubt that though they often competed for authors they were genuinely fond of each other outside of their work.

"Mark, Julie, this is my good friend Annie," Jen introduced them.

"Hey Annie, glad you could make it," Julie was quick to greet her new guest.

"Thank you so much for the invite," Annie replied, hoping her voice wasn't actually shaking from nerves. "Your home is just beautiful!"

"Thanks. Tell you what," Mark smiled, "why don't you all go off and chat while I cook."

"I guess we're being dismissed," Julie complained lightheartedly as she waved her hand as if acknowledging that he was brushing them aside. "Let's go in the kitchen and grab ourselves a drink."

"I'm for that," replied Jen, grinning.

"If you don't mind, I'm just going to dip my toes in the water, I haven't been to the beach in forever. But whatever you're having I'll have one too!" Truthfully Annie's stomach was in knots. She was afraid to go inside the house. She needed to get away and gather her thoughts. She knew he was here. Not that she'd spotted him yet, but she just had that feeling. She'd dressed for the holiday, beach style in a flowing white gauzy skirt and navy blue light cotton shirt with a red scarf tied around her waist as a decorative belt, which she could use later when the sun went down. Luce and Jen had served as fashion consultants the night before, making sure that she'd be up to the task should Chris be there. Thankfully it was the perfect outfit for a stroll along the water line. She imagined him somewhere in the distance, spotting her from afar. Running towards her. Oh sweet Jesus, she was never going to make it through this day with her imagination in overdrive.

As Julie and Jen headed into the kitchen Jen let out a small gasp, and quickly coughed to cover it up. Julie looked over at her curiously, but then seemed to pay no attention.

There in all his splendor was Chris. Yep, just as gorgeous as she remembered. This was definitely the man she'd met last year. She looked about discreetly, hoping Annie was still outside at a distance.

He was looking at Jen a little too closely, and she felt herself flush. Please don't let him recognize me, she begged silently.

"Hey, Chris" Julie called out, "Meet my friend Jennifer Stoltz."

Chris held out his hand politely, "Nice to meet you Jennifer."

"Call me Jen," she replied with a small smile.

Chris tipped his head slightly and looked at her with an odd expression. "Do I know you from somewhere?"

"Um, no, not exactly. I don't think so, unless you're a writer? Maybe that's how we met."

"Actually I'm a chef. So that's not likely." And he smiled, and it seemed to Jen there was a gleam in his eye. Like he knew she knew. But that was silly.

"You're right. Anyway, I'm in the same business as Mark, so we travel in the same circles. We've probably just run into each other."

"I suppose," replied Chris, again, his eyes definitely sparkling with what could only be considered humor.

Just as Jen thought she couldn't feel more awkward, Mark came in with a tray carrying what might have been burgers, might have been hockey pucks. Hard to tell.

"Ah I see you've met my buddy Chris Gregory."

"Yes we were just introducing ourselves," Jen kept her head turned slightly. She couldn't let him see her expression. My god, it was really him, no doubt.

"Great. Now if you two will excuse us, Julie and I have some shrimp to grill," and with that the two departed leaving Jen and Chris in the kitchen.

As soon as they'd left, Chris looked over at Jen, smiling softly, the humorous glint still in his eyes. "Not gonna rat me out, are you?" he asked softly. Jen narrowed her eyes and looked up at him curiously. He couldn't possibly know what she was thinking, or why she'd rat him out. She tried to play it cool. "You mean that you're a chef who secretly attends writing symposiums?" she tipped her head and smiled. "No, I don't think I will. I didn't know if you remembered me."

"Of course," he replied, grinning now. "You were a good listener, as I recall."

"That's what I'm told," Jen laughed, taking him by the arm, "come on handsome chef, let's go mingle. Your secret's safe with me." Inwardly, she breathed a sigh of relief. She was treading in deep water here. If he discovered what she really knew, he'd avoid her like a plague.

As they stepped outside, she surveyed the scene. She needed to spot Annie and keep her away for just a few minutes more. She needed some alone time with this guy. She needed a game plan. Or maybe not. Maybe she had him right where she wanted him.

"Why don't we grab those chairs over there before they're snatched up by someone?" she kept her tone light and friendly. Nodding his head in agreement, he let go of her arm and briskly walked over to claim the seats. Grabbing one, he patted the other seat, indicating she should take it.

She sat down, turned to him, ready to start her inquisition, when she felt a shadow looming. *Uh oh.*

She watched Chris's face as it went from relaxed to surprised to what could only be described as shock. Looking up over her shoulder, she saw the same stunned look on Annie's face, and knowing neither was paying a bit of attention to her, she slipped out of the chair murmuring a soft "if you'll excuse me," and headed towards the barbecue.

The silence was pretty much deafening. They continued to simply stare at each other.

Annie could not take her eyes off him. His strong, handsome features were even more refined, and his body was definitely holding up well. Tall, lean and muscular with those oh-so-broad shoulders. He hadn't really changed at all. It was as if the last 5 years had simply been a blip in time.

"Hey," Chris decided to break the silence.

"Hey back," Annie replied, still not moving.

"This is unexpected." And that was a stupid thing to say Chris thought to himself.

"Who were you expecting, the queen?" Annie's reply was equally ridiculous.

Chris sighed. "Maybe you could sit, and we can start again?" Chris was still trying to fathom how Annie was here. Here. The last place on earth he could ever envision running into her.

Annie sat down, silently cursing the lounge chairs that made it so damn hard to be dignified. She perched on the side of the chair, considering whether she should just bolt or stick it out.

"OK, I'm game Chris. Why are you here?" Play dumb she thought. Best thing.

"Mark's a good friend," Chris replied. Whew, he thought. At least it was true. "And you?"

"My friend Jen needed a last-minute date," Annie replied. "She hates going places alone." Sooo not true, but hey.

"Been a long time, Annie."

"Too long," it came out before she could stop it.

"Yeah, too long," Chris replied not taking his eyes off her for even a second. The effect of the setting sun reflecting off the water behind her created an ethereal effect. But he wasn't dreaming. He was wide awake, and she was real.

He glanced at her hand, he couldn't help it. He had to know. *No Ring.* Looking back up at her face, his look softened a bit.

"Not married?"

"Nope."

"Divorced?"

"Never married."

Chris sighed. "I'm sorry. Really. What happened?"

Annie shrugged. "Larry, my fiancé, he slept with Nora."

"Well shit, then he wasn't worthy. I'm glad you didn't marry him."

"Me too." She glanced down at his hand, doing her own ring-check. "I take it you aren't married? The girlfriend. What happened to her?"

He shrugged as if that answered her question.

"So still in New York?" He changed the subject quickly and they spoke quietly for a few more minutes, about nothing much, superficial things. Nervous chatter. Annie wanted to ask him point blank if he was the author C.A. McLain, and Chris was desperate to know if Annie had read the book. But neither spoke up. Somehow their fear once again got in the way. Neither was willing to break the seemingly magical spell by dredging up the past.

"Take a walk with me?" Chris stood and held his hand out for her to take. Holding his breath that she would.

Annie took a deep breath, looked up at Chris, nodded, and took the hand he offered figuring he was just helping her out of the chair. Always the gentleman, she thought. Or maybe he just remembered her lack of grace and coordination and was making sure she didn't have to struggle to get up. There is nothing like a chaise lounge to turn even a ballerina into a klutz.

But when he didn't let go, she didn't either, and they headed toward the beach, hand in hand as if it were the most natural thing on earth. She kind of wanted to slip her sandals off, and go barefoot but that would require letting go of his hand, and there was no way on earth that was going to happen. She tried to act calm cool and collected but that simply wasn't possible. She stole a glance at Chris, and fleetingly saw a sense of vulnerability in him too. So he wasn't so unaffected by this either. Just that little bit of knowledge gave her the burst of courage she needed.

"So where's home for you now, Chris?" she figured she'd start light, as it wasn't yet time for the Spanish Inquisition.

"Well, kind of complicated, but" Chris started to weave an answer together when Annie's phone buzzed.

"Go on," she said, ignoring it.

"Might be important, go ahead," Chris prodded her to check her phone, perhaps she'd forget she asked. Not that he didn't want her to know where he lived, he simply didn't want to start explaining why.

"Fine, I'll check my message," she sighed for emphasis. She knew without a doubt he was stalling. Grabbing her phone from her shoulder bag, she looked quickly at the screen, assuming it was Luce asking for an update.

Didn't I tell you to back off? Didn't I?

Annie's face turned pale as she stared at the message. She quickly swiped to erase it, somehow knowing it might not be a wrong number after all, but out of sight out of mind. Nobody was going to ruin this for her. Nobody.

"What's wrong?" Chris's voice was laced with worry. He could see something had just frightened her.

"Nothing, it's nothing. Just some creep with the wrong number." There. That's all it was. Saying it out loud helped.

"You sure? You don't look so sure. What did it say?"

"Nothing. It's fine. Forget it." She knew it wasn't fine but right now, it just didn't matter.

Chris knew how creepy text messages could be. He'd had his share of nutty fans over the years.

"Do you get a lot of those?" Chris couldn't help but wonder. It had been a long time, who knew what Annie was into now.

"Just forget it Chris, ok? Now, where were we. Oh right, you're living where?" It was kind of fun hanging on to this little secret. He had absolutely no idea she suspected he was McLain, of that she was quite sure.

"I'm kind of between places right now, actually," Chris replied, launching into a brief but convoluted tale about multiple properties in a down market that ultimately made little sense. He didn't lie, per se, but he didn't exactly answer her question either. He hated doing it, but this was just not the right time or place to have that conversation. The one they both knew was coming.

Annie chuckled as she listened to him avoiding the question, as she just really didn't care. Standing here at the waterfront, listening to the smooth timbre of his voice was enough. She was happy enough to just to be in this moment with him. If it all went to hell tomorrow, she'd have this one day. It would have to be enough.

######

Jen stepped back out to the patio, and looked over to where she'd left Annie and Chris. Gone. Last time she checked, they were still sitting there, talking, and she could see how they were both sort of leaning into each other as they spoke. Good sign, she thought. Oh did she ever want to go back over and listen in. Not possible of course, she knew that. She'd have to wait for the drive home. It would be torture. Then she spotted them, down by the water. Hand in hand? Oh this was good, Jen smiled to herself. This was perfect.

"Is that Chris and your friend?" Julie's voice was beyond curious coming up behind her. "I don't believe it. I mean, Jen, Chris isn't really a player and seriously didn't they just meet?"

Jen knew she couldn't lie to Julie. It'd come out eventually anyway. She turned and smiled at Julie. "Yes, right on all counts, except one, and there *is* a good explanation. You might want to find Mark though. I'm pretty sure he'll want to hear this."

"Hear what?" Mark appeared as if by magic.

"Why our friend Chris is making the moves on Jen's friend down there on the beach." Julie was grinning. She had no idea what this was, but she was loving it.

"Well I'll be," whispered Mark as he looked over at Jen in disbelief. "I know you asked if I had any single friends, but this is a bit much, no?"

"Sorry, Mark, I know it looks bad." Jen laughed apologetically. "Seriously, they're just holding hands, but I should have clued you in. Now, you don't have to answer this," Jen lowered her voice so she wouldn't be overheard. "Am I right in thinking that Annie's strolling along the beach with C.A. McLain?"

Silence. Jen turned and looked first at Mark, then Julie. And the look on their faces told her everything.

"Would it help if I told you her middle name is Jade?" Jen held her breath, closing one eye as if wishing for the right answer. And then it came.

"Damn." Mark spoke first. "I'll be."

Jen smiled. "That right there, as Bill would say, is Ms. Annie Jade Porter."

"Wow," Mark smiled and shook his head. "This is awesome."

"Jen, maybe you could explain how all this happened?" Julie was eager to learn more. "Obviously your bringing her tonight wasn't just fate. I take it Bill isn't really sick, is he?"

"No, Julie, you're right. Let's just say I was playing a hunch, and I'm sorry I didn't fill you in first. Probably would have been the right thing to do."

"Maybe. But maybe standing out here staring at them is definitely the wrong thing to do!" Julie replied. "Let's have a seat, and definitely another drink, and Jen you can tell us what's what."

Julie and Mark had waited a long time for Chris to find his someone. And he finally had. Right here. This was going to be some story.

Chapter 7

Chris laid back in the chaise lounge chair, alone, and stared up at the stars. He was still stunned at the irony of it. *Annie Porter*. He clenched his fists momentarily, trying to release the tension building up in his gut. They'd just spent hours together. After all this time, nothing had changed. His feelings were as strong and deep as ever. And once they'd both relaxed a bit, their conversation never ebbed. Though they avoided anything meaningful, really. They didn't discuss that fateful trip to Ireland. Or the fact that he was not a Chef, but a writer. They talked about her job. Other places he'd been. Places she'd been. When the small talk ran out, they mingled with the guests, as if they were there together. The whole thing was like stepping into a parallel universe, as Annie had put it earlier. So he gave her his number and he took hers, promising to call so they can go out, while he's still in NY. An actual date. Closing his eyes, he smiled as he thought about her reaction.

"So, I'm in town for a few days. Maybe we can do something before I go back."

"Do something?"

"Yeah, you know, like maybe go out somewhere. Have dinner. Something."

Annie took a deep breath and crinkled her eyes, just the way she used to when she was wondering what he was up to.

"Something. Something like a date, Chris? Are you asking me out on a date?"

"I suppose I am," Chris laughed. "Unless it's a no in which case…"

"It's a yes," Annie replied quickly.

"Ok, then, I'll call you. Tomorrow."

"Ok, then, I'll answer. Tomorrow."

The banter was back. Annie was back. His life was headed back on the right path. As long as he didn't screw it up again.

"Penny for your thoughts," Mark's voice rasped in the darkness.

"Hey."

"Hey yourself," Mark replied as he took a seat at the edge of the bench on the nearby picnic table.

Chris sat up slowly, ran his fingers through his hair, and covered his face with his hands for a moment, as if trying to shake loose his thoughts.

"Quite a party, don't you think?"

"As usual, Mark, stellar."

"Stellar, eh? Look. I think it's time you and I had a chat."

"A chat?" Chris looked at Mark questioningly.

"Yep. A little tête-à-tête if you will."

"I suppose you want to know when I'll start the next book."

"Nope."

"No?"

"No. I want to know about Jade. Tell me about her."

"Read the book."

"Funny. Here's what I think. It's mostly true. You met a girl in college. Maybe her name was Jade. Maybe not. You fell in love. You thought she was the one. Till your best friend burst your bubble."

"That's it," whispered Chris.

"No, that's not it. There's a whole lot more to this. Now, tell me about Annie."

"You noticed Annie, huh."

"You were glued at the hip the entire night, like I wouldn't notice? In all the years we've known each other, that has never happened. And I've introduced you to plenty of women."

"Never one like Annie, I guess."

"Who is she, Chris? And don't bullshit me. This is me you're talking to."

"You wanted to know about Jade? Well, Annie is Jade. Annie Jade Porter to be exact."

"What?" Mark had to keep up the charade of being surprised. "That's your long-lost Jade? The love of your life. She just shows up here, out of the blue?"

"Turns out she and Jen are friends. Jen's husband was sick, so she brought Annie. Fate."

Mark tried to mask his smile. Fate in the form of one determined friend named Jen. And the book.

"So what happened? Details Chris, details. You wrote about this woman in your book, and now here she is in the flesh, and you have that once in a lifetime chance to make it right. So I need to know what happened. Julie and I didn't have much chance to get to know her, though I will say we liked her right off the bat."

"What's not to like? She's amazing. Always has been."

"Chris, this is like pulling teeth. You gotta give me something here."

"OK, we caught up a bit, we're going to go out before I go back. On a date. A real one. And no more platonic BS."

"Did she read the book?" Mark knew she had, but he needed to know if Chris knew.

"I don't know. We didn't discuss it."

"Does she know you're an author?"

"Nope."

"Uh oh."

"I'll tell her. I will. When I see her, we'll talk. We have a lot to discuss, but today wasn't the day for that."

"Ok, Chris, I'm just gonna put this out there. I know you have your version of what happened all those years ago. But you need to keep an open mind. I'm only saying this because I saw you together. Call it a hunch." Mark tried not to give away anything Jen had said, but it was tough.

"What do you mean keep an open mind?"

"I'm saying maybe things didn't happen the way you remember. Maybe you need to discover the truth once and for all."

"So I find out I was wrong, and I get to have my heart broken all over again."

"No you find out you were wrong, and you write another best seller featuring Max Colby and his long lost newly found love."

Chris actually began to smile. "You're nuts, you know that?"

"Maybe, but you and I go way back, and I kind of like you. And Julie adores you and you're our daughter's godfather. Which gives me the right to butt in when I want to. And right now I want to."

"You know if you're wrong, losing her again might just be the end of me. No more books."

"Isn't the point of your damn book that you have to take that chance? I'm your fucking editor, Chris. I know the point. You practically screamed at the end for her to take a chance. Looks like she did. Or fate intervened. Whichever, it's your turn now buddy, so don't screw it up." With that, Mark got up and strode into the house. Purposefully leaving Chris to his own thoughts.

"Hi sweetie," Julie looked up at her husband as he came in the kitchen. She could see the concern in his eyes, and knew he was ticked off about something.

"Mark, what were you and Chris arguing about. I heard you almost yelling."

"I think Chris really is clueless sometimes," Mark replied with a sigh.

"You talked to him about Annie?" Julie asked.

"I did. But I didn't tell him what Jen told us, I'm not going to do that. It's for them to work out. I just hope they do."

Julie walked over and placed her hands on his face and leaned up to kiss his cheek. Leaving one hand there for a moment, she smiled at him. She waited, and slowly a smile appeared.

"That's better. You go on up, and I'll be there soon. We'll leave Chris to brood for a while. He knows where the guest room is."

"Thanks Jules. I'll see you upstairs."

He paused at the bottom of the stairs, turned at looked back at his wife of 9 years. Maybe the fiery passion had mellowed, but he'd die without her. He wanted that for Chris. And If he had to walk on fire to get it for him, he would.

######

Chris was back to being lost in thought, memories flooding back. With all he'd written, he'd still left out just a few bits here and there. Some things were better left unsaid. Though in this case, perhaps that was the whole problem. He smiled as he realized tonight he'd finally landed that date with Annie. He'd asked her out. And she'd said yes. It'd been a very, very long time coming.

He'd always wanted to ask her out. Badly. Since the first time they'd met. But it seemed every time he saw her was a new opportunity he passed on. He'd never had a problem asking a girl out before. I mean you just walk up and say hey, want to go to a movie? But no, somehow, with Annie, he couldn't. Instead he'd organize study groups or some other pretense to see her. Worse yet, whenever there was that moment, the one that screams out go ahead, make your move, something would interfere. Every. Single. Time.

Until at some point their friendship was so established it became impossible to change its trajectory. Other guys came along, not afraid to ask her out. Or kiss her goodnight. Or probably worse.

Chris grimaced as he remembered the time he came upon her coming home after one such date. Too late he realized he was caught witnessing a truly awkward moment. Caught in the hallway just near her dorm room, she was politely trying to disentangle herself from the octopus she'd been out with. He could have intervened. Could have helped. He saw her glance over at him, her eyes pleading with him to do something. He did. He left. Backed away and hurried down the stairs. Not a good move. When he saw her the next day, headed to class, he casually strolled up next to her, intending to walk with her. Instead she gave him a cold hard stare, crinkling her eyes the way she did when she was either angry or suspicious, and stalked off at a faster pace. How was he to know when to step in and when to back away?

They never could get it right he thought. They came close. A few times in fact. He smiled as he remembered getting the letter. He'd entered a contest with a photo series he'd done that summer. He'd gone to the cabin one weekend. There was a storm front moving in and he'd taken the boat out and snapped away. He must have photographed every fish, every insect, every ripple on the water as well as the strange and wonderful cloud formations just coming into view. In the end, he'd chosen a half dozen photos, each one capturing a different essence of the calm before the storm. He won the competition, and earned a photo gig in Ireland as well. It was his first paying job as a photojournalist. And the first person he thought to tell was Annie.

"I did it Annie." Chris was beaming from ear to ear.

"Did what?" Annie mumbled, preoccupied, loading her resumé onto every jobsite.

"I won." Chris sat down on the edge of Annie's chair, nearly causing her to fall off. At least she caught herself sliding and righted herself.

"OK, out with it. Won what?" He had her full attention now.

"The Mother Earth 2009 Young Photographer's award of excellence. That contest I entered."

"Seriously Chris that's amazing!" Annie jumped up, as excited for him as he was for himself. "If anyone deserved it it's you. Those pictures were awesome."

"Yeah and guess what else!"

"What?"

"I got a gig. In Ireland! The Wild Atlantic Coast. I'm a real photojournalist. Not sure what I'll tell my dad of course."

"The truth. You tell him the truth. He'll understand. This is too big to pass up. You know now I'm totally jealous. I've always always wanted to go. You're just going to have to take me with you," Annie teased.

Chris sighed remembering how he had just blurted it out. "OK" he'd said. Just like that. OK. He'd bring her with him.

"It's a deal, Chris, shake on it." Annie laughed as she held out her hand, and Chris had taken it, and they'd stared at each other for what seemed like an hour.

"OK," he'd whispered back. "Deal."

It wasn't to be of course. Oh he had gone to Ireland, but he had gone alone. They'd gotten it entirely wrong that time, and it seems it wouldn't be the last time either.

#######

The drive back wasn't nearly as long without the traffic, as it was close to Midnight, but it gave Jen and Annie plenty of time to hash through every detail. Annie'd called Luce and put her on speaker so she could hear it all too.

"Tell me that part again, when he asked you out. Don't leave out anything," Luce, ever the inquisitive reporter, had to know everything.

"He asked me if maybe I wanted to go out, and I said, what, like on a date, and he said yeah, unless I was gonna say no… but I said yes so fast he couldn't take it back. No way he was squirming out this time."

"Ya know, sis, I'm really happy for you. And if that idiot doesn't call you tomorrow I'm going after him, you know that right?" Luce laughed, but she meant it. No way was she letting this guy hurt Annie again.

"Right there with you Luce," Jen chimed in.

"You'd both have to get in line," Annie chimed in enthusiastically. This time, she wouldn't be played a fool. But if this were going to happen, if they were going to have one more shot at this, she would have to take a risk. One that might just leave her in pieces.

Chapter 8

The gentle rocking of the boat was relaxing, but Chris was too tense to enjoy it. Gazing over at his friend, he wondered if Mark realized how damn lucky he was. He had it all as far as Chris was concerned. A beautiful wife, great kid, great house, great life. It was a life Chris wanted. And it really got under his skin. He could have this. He *should* have this! He hadn't slept at all last night. He'd paced the room, even gone out for a walk on the beach, just trying to ease the tension that had taken over him. Just knowing that Annie was nearby, single, and willing to give this a shot. He was so close and yet so far. He was impatient to see her again. Hold her. Just have her back in his life. But what if she didn't care. Or worse, what if she was out for revenge. Absurd, he knew that. Not Annie. Not ever. Maybe he should call her now. No, text her. He could text her. Just a hello. His nerves were getting the best of him again.

He looked out over the water, his gaze drifting toward a small *for sale* sign stuck loosely in the sand on the shore.

He sat up suddenly, jerking the boat. "Hey Mark. Take us in, over there," he pointed toward the sign.

Mark looked at him curiously. "Sure buddy but can I ask why?"

"I just want to look, okay?" He knew he sounded gruff but didn't care. He was totally focused on the house coming into view through the trees lining the shore.

As they approached, he got the full picture. It was a white colonial, set just a ways back from the beach. It was homey looking, and the wide back veranda was perfect. He could see Annie sitting there. The two of them on a glider watching the boats pass by. Or watching their children play. It was perfect. And it was for sale. As they got to shore, he pulled out his phone and called the number on the sign.

Mark docked the boat and getting out, pulled it ashore with Chris's help. One handed help, but help it was. He said nothing to his friend somehow knowing that whatever Chris was up to, it involved Annie. He'd find out more later. For now he was content to just observe. It almost amused him. There was no doubt that Chris was obsessed with Annie. She must be something, he thought. Because while Chris had dated every so often, he kept all women at arm's length. He and Julie had made more attempts to fix him up than he could count. And no matter how beautiful, intelligent, witty or sophisticated the woman was, Chris never felt anything more than a slight attraction. He'd never seen this side of him. This was definitely a man bitten. And right now he was looking like a man on a mission.

Chris knew as he headed off to meet the realtor in front of the house that he was acting nuts. He hadn't seen Annie again yet. Maybe he wouldn't even get to and here he was already making plans. It was stupid. Completely ridiculous. But right. Deep down right.

Mark waited on the beach, while Chris walked up the makeshift boardwalk to the back lawn of the house and up and around the front. The realtor arrived and Chris was surprised to find the man was pushing 80 if a day. He pulled up in a 65 Olds and Chris had to smile. This was not what he'd envisioned. He'd been expecting a 35-year-old slick salesman in a BMW.

The realtor approached somewhat slowly, but with a bounce in his step Chris thought unusual for a man his age. He was small, thin and wiry, and completely bald. But when he smiled and held out his hand, Chris was instantly relaxed.

"Jake Shall, Mr. Gregory," he spoke first, and quickly went on. "Glad you called. In fact I just put this place on the market. Selling it myself you know."

"So you're *not* the realtor?"

Jake laughed, the crackling sound made Chris smile. "Nope. Those guys want too much money. I'd rather keep it for my grandkids. They may not want this place, but I'm damn sure they want my money when I'm gone."

"You know I'm pretty sure they'd rather have you than the money." Chris smiled at Jake. He liked him and somehow he knew he'd like the house as well.

"Wife and I built this place back after the war. Land wasn't so pricey back then. Though we didn't hurt for much. But it's time to move on. Lost my wife 10 years ago, and my kids are getting too old to keep this place up for me, and the grandkids, well, too busy."

Chris was still pondering the whole "after the war" comment. Korea? Vietnam? Should he ask? Realizing Jake was waiting for some sort of response he blurted out the first thing that came to mind.

"So how much, Jake?" Chris held his breath, though he had enough money, he was sure, he didn't want to go overboard.

"Well, last appraisal was for 1.2, but let's hear your offer." Jake laughed suddenly. "You haven't even seen the place. Tell you what. Come inside, and we'll have a cold drink, look around some."

"Fair enough. Give me a minute to send my friend on his way, and I'll come back and you can show me around." Chris grinned at Jake, then he headed out and back around to the beach.

The tour of the house took longer than expected. Chris couldn't help but pause every few steps to take in the atmosphere. The walls were lined with photos. And they caught Chris's attention. There was Jake and his wife on their wedding day. The expressions of love on their faces unmistakable. Pictures of their children at various ages, and grandchildren. Everywhere in the house was evidence of family. Of warmth. It left Chris feeling empty. He and Annie could have that life. If he had the guts to go for it.

When the tour was complete, Jake led them to the back porch, and waved at Chris to sit in one of the high back Adirondack chairs.

"So. Is this what you're looking for?" Jake asked bluntly.

"It's perfect," Chris replied with a resigning shrug. Jake could see far more though in his face. He was going for nonchalant but the yearning in his eyes was evident.

"Why don't you tell me?" he asked, again, bluntly.

"Tell you?" Chris looked confused.

"Yeah, whatever it is that makes you want this house. Whatever it is that's eating you up inside." Jake smiled warmly. "I've been around, Mr. Gregory. I've seen just about everything. And from where I'm sitting, you want what I've got here, and you want it pretty badly. And I'm not talking about the house."

Chris widened his eyes in surprise. He'd never expected this old man to be so perceptive. And without thinking, he began talking. He left nothing out. In fact, he included all the things he'd left out in his book. Something about the intent way Jake listened drove him on. And when he was done, he leaned back, closed his eyes and took a deep breath. "That's it Jake. The long sad tale."

Opening one eye, he looked over at Jake, who was leaning back in the chair, filling a pipe with tobacco, gently packing it. He smiled at Chris. "Kids won't let me do this up at their place," he winked as he chuckled.

Lighting the pipe, he puffed several times and looked thoughtful.

"OK then," Jake spoke slowly. "Let's have ourselves a talk. Starting with why you want the house."

"Didn't I just tell you?" Chris wondered if maybe he was a bit senile.

"No. You told me your sorry ass tale about letting her get away. What you didn't tell me is why this house. Why now?"

"I don't know," Chris spoke truthfully. "It just feels right. I need to do this." He shrugged. "I know it's not much of a reason, is it? But then again, who knows why some things just seem to fit. This house fits. It was meant for us."

"Good enough, it's yours, if you can swing for it."

Chris smiled. "Don't you want to hear my offer first?"

"Nope. I wanted to hear why first. I built this place with love and I can't leave short of that. You'll do. Of course there is one condition."

"And what's that?" Chris smiled, knowing it would be something unusual.

"Call her."

"I will, I promise." Chris shook his head chuckling.

"I mean now, boy. Not tomorrow, not the next day. You got one of those cell phones, right? Use it."

Chris smiled, realizing this man didn't miss a trick.

"Go on, son, call." Jake maintained a firm tone in his voice.

Chris took a deep breath, and dialed. The phone rang several times, before he heard the voice mail kick in.

"Annie, hi, it's Chris. It's tomorrow, so, I'm calling. I thought maybe we could go out later? Maybe tonight? If you're up to it?" he stopped as he saw Jake smiling and shaking his head back and forth, as if to say, no no no. Not like that. "Well, you have the number, just call me back, okay?"

He looked over at Jake, shrugged, and put away the phone. Now it was up to Annie.

######

Jen waited patiently all morning for the phone to ring. She went through the motions of cleaning and tidying. Scolding the kids when necessary, but her mind was totally focused on Annie and Chris. If everything were as it seemed, this was a real-life love story she couldn't resist. When the phone finally rang, she ran and grabbed it, barely keeping herself from tripping over the couch. It wasn't Annie though. It was Luce. And when Jen hung up, she urgently yelled for Bill.

Chapter 9

Annie sat on the edge of the sofa, head in her hands, tuning out all the commotion around her. Her hair tumbled softly around her shoulders. She felt numb. Things like this just didn't happen to her.

"Ms. Porter?"

She heard the voice, but somehow couldn't make the connection to respond. A slight tap on her shoulder. Still she didn't respond.

Whispers. Then louder voices coming from somewhere. The bedroom?

"Got something!" She heard that too, but gave no reaction.

Then the quiet deep male voice again. "Ms. Porter, we need to speak with you. Would you like to go somewhere else and talk?" Without lifting her head, she shook it slowly.

"Annie!"

Luce? Was that Luce?

"Shit! What the hell happened!" Annie looked up this time, to see her sister standing in the doorway. She looked pale. Terrified. Annie had never seen Luce like this. Except once. Only once before. Their eyes met, and suddenly Annie burst into tears. It was real. This wasn't a dream.

"Excuse me, but you'll have to wait outside," the male voice again, firm but gentle. Annie let her gaze roam, trying to find the source. There, by the hallway. He was tall, dark, fierce looking, but when his eyes caught hers she saw more. A determination. She watched as Luce tried to come in the apartment again, but he was blocking her in two short strides.

"No one comes in here. And that includes you. Especially you."

Annie crinkled her eyes in suspicion. Why wouldn't he let her in? God knows, Annie needed her right now. He was a cop, of course. They all were. There were several uniformed officers and then him, dressed in jeans and a t-shirt, must be a detective she thought.

"Look, Officer," Annie cringed, hearing the sarcasm in Luce's voice. "That's my sister and I'm going in, capisce?"

"This, Mzzz Porter," the man responded with the same tone, "is a crime scene. capisce?"

"It's OK Luce, I'm coming out, I can't be in here right now." Annie rose slowly, almost in a daze and headed out to the corridor with Luce.

"Don't wander too far ladies, we've got some things we need to ask you about," the deep voice called back, this time the sarcasm gone.

"God Annie, what the hell happened?" Luce grabbed Annie's arm and drew her over to the wall to support her.

Annie just looked at Luce for a moment, tears welling up again. "I went to the store. Just needed some bagels and coffee. I was out. So I went to the store," her voice trailed off as she repeated herself.

Luce gave her a reassuring squeeze of her hand. "Go on."

"I came back. Up the stairs. The door was open. I stopped, dropped the bag on the floor, then I don't know, I had this horrible feeling, I was terrified. I knew someone had broken in. I just knew it wasn't you, you never leave the door open. Ever" Annie looked away, into space. "I called 911 from my cellphone. These two cops came and when they opened the door further I saw, well, this," and she pointed at her apartment and spread her arms for emphasis. "They trashed my place, Luce. Totally trashed it. Why? I don't have anything. Why would someone do this?"

"What did they take, Annie?" Luce reverted to the journalist in her.

"I don't know. I just" they were interrupted then.

"Ms. Porter, can I have a word with you?"

The lion man again, Annie thought as she looked at him. His skin was darker, tanned, his eyes almost black, she noticed, but his mane of thick golden hair completed the picture.

"Look Officer Holman, can you lay off her for just one more minute?" Luce spit out.

"No, I can't. And it's Detective, if you don't mind. And I don't want you interrogating her either. This isn't a news story, it's a crime."

Luce bit back a retort, not wanting to antagonize him. Not that her mere presence wasn't doing that.

"Ms. Porter, my name is Detective Holman. I need to ask some questions. Are you up to it?" His voice had that gentle soothing tone again, like melted butter, Annie thought.

"I suppose," Annie replied softly, looking curiously from her sister to the remarkable looking cop.

"Do you guys know each other?" That last part popped out before Annie could stop it.

"We've met, dear sister, remember the night you bailed me out?"

Annie looked at her in surprise, then switched her gaze to the detective.

"You? You arrested my sister?" Annie's tone was firm now, the terrifying haze lifting as she was diverted.

The Detective sighed. "Yes, but it was a misunderstanding and we cleared it up. Your overzealous sister has a habit of invading crime scenes." Annie watched with interest as the side of his mouth curled up, as if he was biting back a smile. Interesting, she thought. Definitely interesting. The sparks flying from these two could ignite a forest fire.

"Ms. Porter," he continued.

"Could you just call me Annie, please?" She interrupted.

"OK. Annie. I need to review what happened, then we'll do a walk through and see what's missing. Can you do that?"

"Sure, OK." Annie braced herself. She'd rather enjoyed the exchange between Luce and him. And she really didn't want to talk about this.

Annie began relaying the events of the morning to the detective. When finished, he began asking more pointed questions. Was she with anyone last night? Did she bring anyone home with her? Was she dating?

A uniformed officer appeared out of nowhere, and whispered something she couldn't hear to the detective.

Annie watched as his face stiffened, and she couldn't be sure, but he looked almost worried.

"Excuse me ladies, stay put, I'll be right back."

He accompanied the officer back into the apartment, leaving Luce and Annie alone. Almost alone. There were two cops stationed in the hall, one at each end. But they were definitely out of earshot.

"OK Luce, what gives. There's more to this between you two than meets the eye." Annie's face was a mask, still pale, but the grin was in her voice.

"What's to say? He's the cop that busted me on that kidnapping case."

"I realize that, but I have a feeling there's far more to the story you never told me. "

"Well, tell you what, tonight, at my place, where by the way you'll be staying, we'll crack open a bottle and talk about it. And, you are going to tell me every single thing about last night."

"Agreed," Annie replied. "You, me and a bottle, actually make that two, of your best vino. It'll take my mind off," she waved her arms in the air, "all this."

The Detective returned, and the stone mask on his face was back in place. "Annie, I need to walk you through here now. There are some things that might disturb you, and I want you to be forewarned. I want you to be alert for things that might be missing, ok? And I have to caution you not to touch anything unless I say so, they're still gathering evidence."

Annie nodded, and started to follow him.

"I'm coming in with her, and don't even think of stopping me," Luce chimed in as she swung her arm over Annie's shoulder protectively.

Detective Holman gave an exaggerated sigh, and shrugged. "Just don't touch a damn thing," he muttered.

"I heard that!" Luce said quickly.

He turned and glared at her, then turned back to lead them in.

The apartment was a wreck. Chairs were knocked over, her knick knacks on the shelves knocked to the floor, many broken. Sofa Pillows were ripped open. The kitchen was no better…the food in the fridge dumped out on the kitchen floor. Her bedroom dresser trashed…all the drawers pulled out and the contents spilled everywhere.

They walked into the bathroom, Annie almost in shock at the destruction so far, but nothing prepared her for this. The mirror over the sink.

The words "Back Off" scrawled in red lipstick. It was like a scene from a movie. Only Annie wasn't involved in anything sinister. She gasped and nearly dropped to the floor. Only Luce's steady hand kept her from falling.

"That's what the texts said," Annie whispered.

"What texts?" The detective was on high alert now.

"I thought it was a wrong number," she whispered still. Terrified really.

A strange look passed between Holman and Luce. "Get her outta here," he said softly, and Luce led her back to the living room.

Luce led Annie back to the sofa, and with a nod from the Detective, they sat down and waited. He came over and kneeled down in front of Annie, focusing his attention on her face, his eyes softened. Luce could grudgingly concede he was good at his job.

"Annie, I need to ask some more questions. First, can you show me the texts?"

"I don't know, I think I deleted them," she said almost apologetically. Reaching for her phone, she scanned her recent messages. "Sorry, I did."

"It's ok, but maybe you can let my guys take a look at your phone, see if we can't retrieve them, ok?" He was pretty sure they could, thankfully.

"Did you notice anything missing? Jewelry, money, that kind of thing?"

"No," Annie whispered softly.

Holman nodded. "Good, that's good."

"Does anyone else have a key to your apartment?"

"Just Luce, though she always forgets it so I keep one under the mat for her."

The detective shook his head in disbelief, as Luce rolled her eyes.

"You do realize that it's the first place anyone looks for a key, right?" he asked.

"Yeah well this is supposed to be a secure building in a safe neighborhood," Annie replied defensively.

Annie looked up suddenly, her eyes wide, and began gazing around her, patting the cushions and looking behind the sofa frantically.

"What is it Annie?" his tone was direct and level. He needed to keep her focused.

"My book," she whispered, her eyes glazing with worry. "Where's my book?" she whispered urgently.

He looked over at Luce for guidance. "Where did you leave it Annie?" Luce asked her gently.

"Right here on the table. Right under the lamp. Where it used to be I mean," she said, gazing down at the smashed remnants of her favorite ceramic lamp base on the floor.

"It's just a book Annie, you can get another copy. I'll give you mine." Luce kept her tone light.

She looked frantic. "You don't understand. It's not the book. I put his picture in there. It's all I have. It's gone. Where is it?" her voice became loud and demanding.

Detective Holman stood up to his full height and quickly took control.

"Tell me about the book and the photo Annie," He looked down at her, commanding her to focus. But she couldn't.

"Detective," Luce's voice bore no hint of sarcasm now. "I'll tell you. Let's move over there though. Annie, sit tight, sweetie, we'll find it, ok?"

Annie nodded, tears falling once again. Leaning back on the sofa, she closed her eyes. This is not happening. It's a dream. I will wake up soon. She silently chanted a mantra.

They left Annie on the sofa and headed to the hallway outside.

"OK, Ms. Porter, let's hear it," he started right in.

"Do you think you could call me Luce?" she smiled as she said it, trying to relieve the tension that always seemed to be present around them.

"OK, Luce…and you can call me detective…" he almost grinned when he said it. Luce's blood pressure jumped. When this man smiled he was a god, she couldn't help thinking.

"Detective?" The voice crackled over Holman's walkie talkie unit.

"Yes?" he responded quickly, holding the button down and releasing it.

"There's a Bill and Jen Stoltz down here, wanting to come up there."

He looked at Luce, the unspoken question in his eyes.

Luce nodded. "They're our friends, well Jen is really Annie's friend, but of course we're all friends. I'm babbling aren't I? How odd. I don't babble. Anyway, they'd never hurt Annie, in fact, they are involved in all this as much as we are. I called them after Annie called me."

"Have them wait in the lobby down there, I'll talk with them in about 20 minutes," he gave the order brusquely, and looked at Luce pointedly. "Involved?" One eyebrow lifted. "Start talking, Luce."

She began by explaining the book, and what they'd been up to lately. He hit the mic on his tablet to record everything she said, freeing him up to multitask. Every so often he'd hold up a finger to pause her running commentary, and call over an officer and ask him or her to check something in the apartment. Her eyes narrowed at one point.

"What?" he asked.

"Well, I just realized. Remember that list of names I told you about?"

"Sure," he replied, "they're looking for it now."

"Well, they won't find it."

"What do you mean?" he asked suspiciously. Something about Luce always made him suspect the worst.

"I put it in the book, in the back."

"I thought you said it was in the drawer of the stand by the door."

"It was, originally, but I just remembered that the other day we were looking it over and I was too lazy to go back to the drawer and I shoved it in the book."

Detective Holman let out an exasperated sigh. "So our one major clue is gone," he muttered.

"Come on, Detective, it was our list. If we can do it once we can do it again."

"I thought you were a reporter, Luce?"

"I was, now I'm a producer, what of it?"

"As a reporter you should realize whoever has that list could use it to hurt someone else. If this is at all related to the book, it may be more of value to our perp than it was to you."

Luce drew back, surprised. "Damn, I didn't think of that. You're right." She laughed ruefully. "Guess I wasn't much of a reporter… eh?"

"I'm not arguing that point, Luce, you sucked." He shook his head in frustration.

"Look, go in there and sit with your sister. I've got some calls to make. Can she stay with you for a while? It's gonna be a few days before we can let her come back, and you'll want to get a cleaning crew in after that as well."

"No problem there. I've got plenty of room, and she's my sister after all. You know it's just the two of us now, well maybe you don't know," she paused as he seemed to look confused. "What? You thought I'd let her go to a hotel?"

He shook his head in wonder. Why they couldn't seem to have a normal conversation bugged him.

"What do you mean, just the two of you?"

"We lost our parents a few years ago," Luce sighed. "Car accident. My job now is to look out for Annie."

"Luce, I'm sorry about your folks… but your sister is a grown woman, right?" "There's nothing you're not telling me… that I need to know?" He wondered if maybe Annie had mental health issues or something else he needed to understand.

"Oh for god's sake, no, she's fine."

"Detective?" Luce's voice was serious now. "I know my investigative skills are worthless, but this does appear to be some sort of 'crime of passion' don't you think?"

"For once, Luce, your instincts are right. It's got all the earmarks. Which is why I don't want your sister to be alone. I want someone with her at all times. Got it?"

"Got it. But I'll have to enlist some help."

"OK, but clear them with me first. And she's not to try and contact this McLain guy, understood? Under no circumstances."

"You don't think he could possibly have done this, do you?" Luce was worried. Maybe this guy was a creep and Annie didn't know. Until last night she hadn't seen him in years anyway.

"I don't think anything yet. But everyone is a suspect Luce, everyone. You should know that much by now. Are we clear?"

"Aye aye captain," Luce smirked.

"That's detective, Luce, de-tec-tive." And he turned and left her standing there, still reeling from the grin that had broken out on his face.

Chapter 10

Mark put down the phone and looked over at Chris. "That was a Police Detective, from the city." He took a deep breath, he couldn't lie to Chris, but he knew Chris would freak. And they hadn't divulged much to him anyway.

"He said they're investigating a break-in, and want to come out and talk to us." The detective hadn't been very forthcoming. They'd only called him because they wanted to confirm the identity of C.A. McLain, and present location, and Mark was the only one who could give it to them. When he asked why, the detective evaded the question.

"Why us? That makes no sense." Chris looked at Mark curiously.

"He didn't say, Chris, just wanted me to verify who you were, and whether you were here. That's all I know."

"Well I certainly haven't left your house except this morning and I don't even know anyone in the City. Except Annie," he paused. "You don't think it's Annie do you? She hasn't called me back you know. I've had my phone on the whole time." Chris jumped up and started pacing around the Sunroom where they'd been relaxing earlier.

"Maybe you should call Jen. She'll know if something's happened. I mean we just can't sit here and do nothing. What if it is Annie and maybe she's hurt? Or worse?" Chris's mind started reeling with possibilities and none of them were good.

Mark quickly dialed Jen's number. "Voice mail," he said to Chris.

"Hey, Jen, Mark, give me a call will you?" Mark disconnected and looked over at Chris.

"I guess we'll just have to wait. Maybe this guy will tell us." Mark tried to remain the calm one, but he was nervous. This whole thing could blow up into a PR nightmare. Though that was the last thing he cared about at the moment.

"Why do they need to talk to us, anyway? Or me. I don't get it. Though now of course *I* want to talk to *them*. I need to know what's going on."

"Whatever happened, whoever it happened to, something is linking it to you. I don't know what that is. Fact is, Chris, I have no clue about any of this. When this Detective gets here we can find out more. For now, let's just have a drink and relax. There's not much else we can do. I have a feeling they called when they were already halfway here so shouldn't be long."

Just then, Mark's phone buzzed, looking down, he spoke aloud. "It's Jen, hang on, I'll put it on speaker."

"Jen? Mark, what's going on?"

"Someone broke into Annie's, don't worry she's fine, and we're not sure what's going on but Luce called me and we raced right over there. We waited down in the lobby, they finally asked us a bunch of questions and then told us not to talk to anyone."

"So you called me," Mark had to smile at that. "Thanks Jen, the cops are on their way here, I don't know what for, but at least now we have something to go on. And glad she's ok. We'll talk later, thanks." Mark disconnected, and saw Chris almost in panic mode.

"Relax buddy."

"Relax? Yeah right. Annie Porter," he held up his hand to stop Mark from saying anything, "is being terrified by someone, or something, which somehow seems to involve me, and you want me to relax."

"Yeah. Or at least try to." Mark looked apologetically at his friend, knowing it didn't make a difference what he said. Chris was wound tighter than a drum. But one thing was now for certain. From the look on his face, Annie Porter was the missing piece of Chris's life. No doubt.

When the bell rang, Chris jumped up to answer it. Mark put out a hand to stop him. "My house, remember? I'm supposed to answer the door. Just settle down," Mark said as he gently pushed Chris back towards the living room.

Chris waited, hearing whispering in the foyer. Tapping his fingers on the arm of the sofa, he began running it all in his mind. Rewinding the events of the past two days. What if it wasn't coincidence that Jen had brought Annie. Or even that she knew Annie. Maybe Jen knew who he was already. But how? The writer's conference? Mark certainly would never betray him. Annie? Did she know? Maybe she'd read the book, figured it out. No way. If she had, she'd have found him come hell or high water just to make him suffer for writing it. She'd never been timid about expressing herself. But why was her apartment broken into? And how could it possibly involve him? Suddenly he stood up and strode toward the foyer. He wasn't going to sit and wait anymore. Maybe the cops wanted to question him, but he had questions of his own.

"Mr. Gregory? Detective Andy Holman, NYPD." Holman stuck his hand out as Chris approached and grasped his in a firm shake. The two men paused, sizing each other up.

Mark spoke up. "Look, why don't we go in and sit down, get comfortable."

"Good idea," the Detective replied quickly, and followed them into the living room.

"Julie?" Mark called out. "Can you bring some iced tea? Please?" Almost got into trouble on that one.

He turned to the detective. "Can I get you something to eat? I'm guessing you missed lunch." Mark had read enough cop novels to know that they're much more agreeable on a full stomach.

"As a matter of fact, I'm starving." Detective Holman smiled at Mark, putting him at ease. "Look, I know you're both wondering what all this is about. I need to ask you both some questions. Some fairly personal. We're investigating a break-in this morning. It was a pretty nasty one. And, a connection has been made to the victim and you, Mr. Gregory, as well as you Mr. Simeon, in a roundabout way of course. I just need to clarify some issues, that's all.

"What do you mean by nasty? And we are talking about Annie, aren't we? I already know we are. Is she ok? I need to know that she's ok!" Chris stood and paced, waiting for the detective's response.

"Yes, we're talking about Annie Porter. And just how you know that is something we'll get to in a moment. Her apartment was ransacked this morning, Mr. Gregory. Totally destroyed almost everything she owned." The detective watched his face, and his body language, for any reaction.

Chris was stunned, even though he'd expected it. The confirmation threw him.

"But she's OK? She wasn't hurt, was she?" Chris demanded.

"She's shaken, but fine." He paused, carefully considering how much information he should feed him. "She wasn't home at the time. She came home and discovered the place trashed."

"And?" Chris knew there was more.

"And I'm afraid that's all I can tell you. Now it's my turn to ask questions, okay?" He tried to smile and soften the harsh tone. He couldn't be sure about Chris yet, but he could turn out to be a key to the whole investigation. Better to keep him calm.

Julie's interruption with the drinks, and thankfully for the Detective, snacks, was welcome. Gave Chris a chance to breathe. And relax, if only slightly.

"First, just to clarify, for the record, you are acquainted with Annie Porter, correct?"

Chris nodded, rolling his eyes at the stupidity of the question. Obviously he was, or the cop wouldn't be here.

"How long have you known each other?"

"I don't know, 15 years, maybe more? We met in college. Her freshman year. It was a long time ago."

"When was the last time you spoke to her?"

"Yesterday, detective, but that was the first time in about 5 years. I guarantee it won't be another 5 though."

"Did you have some sort of falling out? 5 years is a long time."

"Let's just say our signals got crossed."

"Cryptic, but we'll move on for now. I've already confirmed with Mr. Simeon that you are in fact, C.A. McLain. Is that correct?"

"Yes," Chris replied. "Why?"

"Just confirming the facts, Mr. Gregory."

He could see that Chris was agitated. And it would only get worse. But he could also see that Chris didn't appear to be involved with the break-in at all. In fact, his gut instinct was that this guy would jump in front of a train for Annie Porter. And whatever signals got crossed, it looked like they might be uncrossing. One last thing though.

"Can I see your phone, Mr. Gregory?"

"Can I ask why?"

"Just want to verify a few things, if that's all right with you. You don't have to. Your choice." He made it clear in his tone, that if this guy wants to help Annie, he'll hand it over, and so he did, unlocking the screen first so the Detective could scroll through.

After checking the phone's log and the number, Holman was fairly certain Annie's mystery text didn't come from there. But he did notice one detail worth noting. The area code matched the threatening text messages. Ohio.

"Where do you live Mr. Gregory?"

"I split my time between Ohio and New York."

He questioned Chris for over an hour. Then Mark, then Julie too. By the time he was done, it was all coming together. The book was the focus. That was clear. He had read it actually, and grinned as he drove away from the Simeon's house. It was a great book, and now that he could place the characters, it was even better. And he was betting he was one of the few people in the world who now knew who C.A. McLain was. And who the muse was for his latest heroine. Of course Gregory hadn't come right out and said it, but it was right there in his report, Ann "Jade" Porter. He wasn't a big believer in coincidence. And while the author had also insisted they'd been nothing but friends, it was clear after meeting and interviewing both Annie and Chris that their feelings went far deeper. And someone, in their past or present, isn't happy about it.

It had been tough to keep information from Chris Gregory. He knew the guy was probably totally frustrated. In fact normally he would have questioned him alone, and provided no information at all, but he knew that there were too many moving parts in this scenario and containing the flow of information was up to him. So far, all the alibis were checking out and his gut told him Chris could be removed from the suspect list.

Didn't mean he wanted him anywhere near the victim for now. In fact, Chris practically exploded when he informed him he couldn't try to get in touch with Annie yet. Ironically, it had been tough to get the normally reclusive author to agree to drop out of sight for a while. He'd had to convince him that his hanging around would endanger Annie. No calls, no texts and definitely no personal contact. Not easy to do, since he couldn't divulge any of the circumstances. The poor man seemed completely baffled by the whole thing. This was going to take time to sort out. And whoever was behind this was emotionally invested, and therefore, dangerous.

Now he'd have to sort through the list of people Luce talked about. Or the lack of a list. He needed to meet with her, and it looked like he'd need to stop by her place tonight to do it. At least Annie would be there too. Just the thought of he and Luce trying to cooperate with each other was a joke. Hopefully Annie could mediate. This was not a typical B&E and for Andy Holman, there was nothing better than a good mystery. Even if Luce Porter were involved. Especially if Luce Porter was involved.

Chapter 11

Luce peered through the hole, and seeing who it was, opened it, a look of exasperation on her face.

"Whatever it is, detective, it's going to have to wait."

"What? No hello? How are you?" Detective Holman answered quickly.

"Hello. How are you. There. Now you can go."

"Uh uh. I need to talk with you and Annie," he replied shaking his head.

"Annie is in no condition to talk."

That got his attention. "What's happened? Nobody paged me!"

Luce looked chagrined for a moment. "Um, she's OK. She's just, well, she's about 3 sheets to the wind, Detective," Luce looked away, embarrassed. He really was concerned, and she'd had no right to mess with him.

"How about we drop the detective, and you call me Andy. And drunk or not, I still need to talk with you both."

"I don't see what you're going to accomplish," Luce was miffed now.

"Quite a bit, more than likely, because she's probably relaxed enough to let down her guard, and speak freely. First rule of good investigative work, Luce." He bit back a smile as he said it. It was just too much fun goading her.

"Hey! Lucey goosey, who's at the door? Invite 'em in and we'll have a party!"

Andy couldn't help but laugh out loud. Luce was stunned. She hadn't heard him laugh before. And it was a deep, throaty laugh that sent chills through her body. She blushed, trying to banish the wicked thoughts in her head. Looking away, she pretended to be searching out Annie. She turned back and waved him in. Closing the door behind him he took a quick look around. Definitely Luce's touch. No doubt. It was sparsely furnished, but what she did have was first class all the way. Elegant, and totally Luce. Not exactly a kick back and put your feet up kind of place, but it would do. Andy enjoyed being comfortable, but he'd been raised with old money and never could really shake the upper crust out of his system.

He followed Luce toward the living room, and found Annie sprawled on her back on the hardwood floor, a glass of wine in her hand. Lifting her head slightly, and waving the glass around, wine perilously sloshing about, she grinned.

"Lookey here! If it isn't our friend the Ocifer! Hey Detective, looking good! In fact you looked pretty good this morning, but that leather bomber really does something for you." Scrunching her face up she looked suddenly baffled. "Isn't it a little warm out for a jacket?" Laying her head back down, she closed her eyes and sighed. "If I weren't so obsessed with a certain idiotic author, I'd jump your bones. Then you'd probably arrest me for assaulting an officer. I'd end up in jail. A perfect end to a perfect day."

"Well as good as that offer is, Annie, I'm going to have to pass, as I'm here on official business," he replied good-naturedly. Andy chuckled and looked over at Luce, who was looking a little peaked.

"I'd like to put together that list of people, if you think you're up to it."

"I can do that, can't I Luce?" Annie didn't open her eyes, or move. "I just seem to be a little stuck, though."

Luce strode over, trying to remain composed. "Come on sis," she said reaching down to pull her upright. "Sit up and we'll get this over with."

"Ready anytime, ladies." Andy spoke with a touch of sarcasm. Watching the two of them was like watching a pair of comediennes. "Who wants to go first?"

"That would be me," Annie spoke triumphantly, as she sidled over to lean her head against the ottoman. "OK. Fire away lieutenant!"

"OK," the detective began shaking his head with a small smile. "Let's start with the main characters in this story?"

"Sure. First up would be Chris."

"Chris Gregory, AKA C.A. McLain. Got it." He began writing.

"You know for sure, don't you?" Annie looked at him suspiciously.

"I suppose I would know one way or the other, wouldn't I? It's official police business, after all," he chuckled softly, shaking his head again.

"Ya didn't answer the question." Annie persisted.

"I'm afraid I can't," Andy smiled at her. "But I think you know the answer anyway, don't you?"

Annie beamed back. "I suppose I do."

"Who do you think he is in the book? The Sheriff?"

"Yep. Max Colby is Chris, that's for sure." Annie sighed.

"OK, next?" Andy was back to business.

"Well, Rick would be Sam, Chris's best friend."

"Last name?"

"Peckett."

"Tell me about him."

"Aah, what's to tell. He was quiet, really, a nice guy, not drop dead gorgeous but endearing in a way. Treated me like a sister most of the time."

"Go on."

"Well, Taylor would be Sam's girlfriend, Martha. Martha Stewart!" Annie giggled. "Oops, maybe not, try Martha Ross, yeah that's it, Ross." Annie looked serious for a moment. "Never mind, scratch that. She's dead."

"Dead?" Andy queried.

"Yeah," Annie sighed. "She OD'd a few months after graduation. She liked to experiment with drugs, ya know? Sam said it was suicide, but I think it was accidental."

"Huh." Andy entered the additional information into his tablet and moved on.

"The thing is, she was OK, a little on the butch side if you get my drift. Didn't understand why I liked Chris though. She was always telling me to give it up and go find someone else. Not the most supportive friend."

"Wait, Sam's girlfriend was a lesbian?"

"What? No!" Annie shook her head furiously. "Why would she date Sam if she were gay?"

"You just said she was butch."

"Yeah, you know, tough. Loved Kickboxing, swore a lot."

"Sorry, never heard it used that way before. But OK, moving on."

"Did you consider her a friend?" Andy asked pointedly.

"I suppose. I mean we all hung out. She wasn't a close friend, but friends, yeah. It's really a shame. But it was a long time ago." She sighed again, and thought for a moment. She needed to move away from this subject. It always depressed her. After Martha's death, everything and everyone seemed to change. Sam was morose. Sullen and cranky all the time. Chris was guarded after that. It was probably the turning point for all of them.

"Annie?"

"Hmmm?

"Who else?" Andy tried to refocus her attention.

"Oh well some of them I have no idea who's who. I know they were in the book but," her voice trailed off as she considered.

"Annie, focus here. How about you just tell me who you remember, don't worry about who they are in the book. I'm a detective, I'll figure it out."

Annie leaned back, closing her eyes for a moment.

She did her best to rattle off the same names she'd given Luce, but it was hard right at that moment to keep it all straight. Andy only stopped her when she mentioned her roommate and Chris didn't get along.

"Why? Didn't he like her?" Andy made a note on his pad, he'd have to pursue this.

"Well, those two were like oil and water. They just couldn't stand each other. I never figured out why, and to be honest it was better that way. Everyone but everyone wanted to date Kelsey. I kind of liked the fact that he didn't."

Andy shook his head, recording it all, and Luce just smiled indulgently.

"Have you stayed in touch with her?" Andy pried further.

"I might get a card for holidays, birthdays, that kind of thing. Last I heard she was in Rome, selling shoes."

"Who else?" Andy prodded.

"Well, there's Yvonne. She lived next door. Pretty nice, a little loose, but hey."

"Annie, you were so uptight in college you thought a girl was loose if she kissed on the third date," Luce interjected with a chuckle, causing Andy to look at her in surprise. Turning to Annie, he was intrigued. She was nothing like her sister at all. Andy would bet good money Luce wasn't so timid with men. In fact, no, he wouldn't let his thoughts go there.

"Go on, did she know Chris?" Andy tried to keep her focused, himself as well, but at the same time her rambling might help shed light on each person.

"Oh yeah, she was pretty much my confidant. See as close as Kelsey and I were, she couldn't understand why I didn't, well, you know, go after Chris harder. Being so perfect, she just didn't have a clue. Yvonne would hear me out, give me advice, that kind of thing."

"Ya know, speaking of *experience*" Annie shook her head to clear it, and waved her glass around again, making Luce cringe, before continuing. "We should put Nora on the list!"

"Nympho Nora?" Luce asked, smiling despite herself.

"Yep. Good old Nora," she sighed.

"OK," Andy interrupted, "who's Nora?"

Luce glanced over at Andy, seated on the sofa, and it struck her that he looked just like he belonged there. But that wasn't possible. The sofa cost $4,000 and belonged in a penthouse. And he was just a NYPD cop in jeans. He should have looked out of place. Instead, he just fit. His muscular, long, lean legs were stretched out and…she tried to focus back on Annie. This man was just too damn distracting.

"Nora Jacobs. Annie's nemesis from way back." There. She had spoken. Back to normal. For a minute Luce thought she'd lost her mind.

"How far back?" Andy sensed something here.

"Middle School"

"I suppose I don't need to ask why you call her nympho Nora, now do I?"

"Nope!" Annie replied cheerfully. "That bitch slept with every boyfriend I ever had."

"Before or after you dated them?" Andy quickly asked.

"Oh, I don't know…does it matter?"

"It might."

"Well let's see. I think usually she slept with them the minute she thought I was interested. Yep. That about sums her up!"

Andy glanced at Luce, hoping for more.

"Care to add something?" he asked.

"Not much to tell, Det… I mean Andy. Nora was like a bad shadow. Whatever Annie did, wherever she went, there was Nora to poison everything. That bimbo even followed her to school, 500 miles away from home."

He looked at Annie curiously. "Do you stay in touch with her?"

Annie snorted. "Hah! She slept with my fiancé you know."

"Whoa. She what?"

"Like I said, every boyfriend I ever had."

"Yeah but I figured you were kind of exaggerating, sorry." Andy was beginning to get a clearer picture.

"Hmm," he muttered softly. "How long ago was that?"

"5 years, 'tective, 5 years."

Andy paused, made a note. This 5 years was sounding a bit familiar to him.

"Does she have any idea where you are now."

"I don't know, I suppose," Annie looked pensive.

"You don't think, I mean, it's not possible that she'd," Annie was actually sobering up, and she didn't like it.

"Anything's possible Annie." His voice was gentle, but there was a distinct warning to it. He continued to ask about Nora, then decided to move on.

"OK. Let's get some other names down here." As Andy began tapping on the screen quickly to keep up, both Annie and Luce started rattling off names. Occasionally he'd interrupt, trying to get further information.

"So all these people were involved with you and Chris in some way, right?" he asked when they'd finally indicated that was all.

"Yep," Annie replied emphatically. "But I don't think any of them are like, criminals, I mean really," Annie looked at Luce for confirmation. But Luce's expression was thoughtful.

"I don't know, Annie, I only met a few of these people. I can't be too helpful there. You knew them, mostly I just heard about them."

"Look," Andy said. "Someone isn't happy with you Annie, and for now, we need you to lay low so we can sort through it all. That means stay away from anyone on this list, especially Chris Gregory. And if any one of these people suddenly reappears in your life; a phone call out of the blue, maybe you see them in a restaurant or on the street, a surprise email, you let me know."

"Now, how well do you know the Stoltz's?"

"Well, let's see, I met Jen a few years ago, maybe 3 or 4 years? We're pretty tight friends," her voice started to trail off again.

"OK." He turned his attention to Luce.

"Listen, until we have a better handle on this, you can't talk about this with anyone, not even Jen. And Luce, you're going to want to keep an eye on your sister here." He glanced over at Annie, who was back to laying on the floor with her eyes closed. "I think she needs a little watching right about now," his voice laced with humor and concern, he smiled at Luce.

"Well, I'm out of here. Luce, here's my direct number, and my pager number. Anything happens or you think of anything, you get a hold of me right away. Your sister too. Keep this number with you, got it?"

Luce nodded as she took the cards. As Andy got up and approached the door, she stopped him. "Detective?"

He turned back toward her. "Yes?"

"Thanks," she murmured softly. Barely a whisper.

Putting his hand to his ear, he replied. "eh? What's that? Don't think I heard you…" he grinned.

Luce felt herself flushing and bit back a retort. "Goodnight, Detective."

Chapter 12

So far so good. Annie started the car and looked around. *Nope. Not a soul around. Good.* Everything was going smooth. She'd waited till Luce fell asleep, and snuck down to the street, where her rental car was waiting. It was past midnight, so she could get away unseen. She threw her bags in the trunk, threw her purse and cell phone on the passenger seat, got in, locked the door and started the car up. It was muggy, and she cranked the AC to cool her off, and keep her awake. She had a long drive ahead of her. A drive she hadn't made in a very long time.

As she headed toward the bridge, and her salvation, she realized she'd been living with Luce for two weeks. Seemed more like two decades. She couldn't take it anymore. There were no leads on the break-in. She could go back to her apartment anytime, except it wasn't all fixed up yet and she didn't want to be in the way. She couldn't figure out how her life had gone from dull and boring to complete helter skelter. She'd decided to cash in on all that vacation time she'd sat on at work and take a break from all of it. But, she couldn't stop thinking about Chris. She had to see him. Talk to him. She was still being told to lay low and not contact him. And it was making her nuts. She'd known there had to be a way. And then she'd remembered the cabin. She wasn't sure if she could still find the area, but it was worth a shot. She remembered how Chris and his friends would go off on fishing trips, and rave about the incredible cabins people had built up there. They couldn't afford them, naturally, but Chris had always talked about them. "Someday," he'd say, "I'm going to build one right off the lake. It'll be bigger and better than anyone else's. It'll have a loft and a fireplace and a great big porch." Annie shrugged and sighed, remembering how they both used to dream together about what they would do when they made it big. Not that Annie had ever been ambitious, but she did want to succeed at something. But Chris had made it. And he'd let it slip out at the Simeon's party that he'd finally built that cabin. Walking down by the water, he'd mentioned it. She knew without a doubt that it would be somewhere in the vicinity of his favorite spot at the lake, and she was pretty sure she could find it. She'd been up there a few times with him, Sam and Martha. He'd bring his camera and spend most of his time taking pictures. She smiled, remembering how intent he was on getting the perfect shot. Ansel Adams in the making, she used to tease.

Annie looked up at the approaching sign. Cleveland. 360 miles. Only 5 or 6 more hours. It'll be dawn when she gets there. Finding his place will be easier with daylight. Switching on the radio, she hit the tuning button to find something she could stand. It was satellite radio, so at least she didn't have to fight the static. Amazing what technology had done in just a few short years. She settled on a retro station with top hits of the last few decades, and happily sang along, knowing it was dark and no one could see her, feeling buoyed by her plan. And since her phone hadn't rung, seems nobody had noticed she'd left. Yet.

She drove for another few hours before pulling off to take a break. The Interstate was not the most interesting drive, and the boredom was getting to her. She needed to stretch and clear her head. As she pulled off, she noticed the car behind her followed. Don't be paranoid, she thought. Other drivers need to stop too. Everyone has to pee after all. But something nagged her, and after grabbing a coffee and some snacks and filling up with gas, she quickly pulled back onto the highway. And there was someone once again right behind her.

Annie felt the prickly sensation in her neck warning her that something was wrong. OK. So someone was following her. Just keep driving. Ignore them. That nagging feeling was getting stronger though. It was pitch dark out, and the rocky cliffs lining the turnpike were creepy. Signs dotted the roadway warning of crossing deer and falling rocks. There should be one for paranoid drivers, she mused.

Determined, she drove on, picturing the cabin. It would be made of stone and wood, an A-Frame. There would be big picture windows in back, overlooking the water. It would have a warm, cozy feeling to it. Annie breathed a sigh of relief. Only 150 miles to go. More than halfway there, she thought. This had been a monumentally stupid idea to drive through Pennsylvania in the wee hours of the morning, alone. Damn. She had to pee again. She needed more coffee. If she drank more coffee, she'd have to pee again. Vicious cycle. She had lost track of the car that had followed her. Time to pull over. Maybe just a little further, almost there, she could wait.

She drove on determined to get there faster. But ultimately, nature stopped calling and started screaming, and she really needed to stop. Spotting the tall, lit signs off the road, she'd found her spot. She turned on her signal and took the next exit. This time she didn't notice anyone behind her. Until it was too late. The headlights came up behind her, fast and bright, blinding her. The exit road was narrow, only one lane, and the car behind her was too close. Then it pulled to her left to pass. She slowed down. It slowed down with her and started to veer back into her lane. It was coming right at her.

Annie panicked the instant the other car rammed her rear side. She swerved off the road, into a ditch, bouncing from the speed. She couldn't seem to slow down. Somewhere in her brain it registered that the other car had sped off. The scraping of the branches and twigs in the growth terrified her. Suddenly she hit something and the car jerked to a stop.

Annie slowly opened her eyes. The air bag had deployed. Her head was leaning on it. She lifted it slowly and began to try and move around. There was pain in her head and a ringing sensation in her ears. But everything seemed to be working. She must have blacked out. What had she hit? A rock? A tree? How long had she been out? Dazed, she looked at her watch. Thank god it was a tacky glow in the dark one. 6:30. But what time was it before? She couldn't remember. She began to tremble. She'd been scared before, but not like this. Not even the break-in had made her this terrified. 911. She could call them. But where was she? Though the sun was coming up, it was still too dark to see anything. She hadn't looked at the exit sign to see the town. She didn't think she should get out of the car. But what if it caught fire? Was that gas she smelled? Was it leaking? Would the car start? It wasn't running anymore. Had she turned it off?

Her eyes widened as she saw the lights in her rearview mirror. Red and blue…flashing…coming to a stop. The relief was overwhelming. She was safe. For now. But there would be questions. Tell the truth. Who cares. Let them help her. Would they believe her? Or would they call the NYPD and check it out. What if they thought she was drunk? Or worse, on drugs? She'd have to tell the truth. She'd get in trouble. Trouble? She was really losing it. So what. Luce would chastise her. She could deal with that. But Holman the cop wasn't going to just chastise her. He'd explicitly told her NOT to do this. Was she violating some law? Hell no, she was a victim. She had rights too. She saw the flashlight bobbing as someone approached. Sheriff? Highway Patrol? She closed her eyes. Breathe. Just breathe.

The flashlight tapped on her window, startling her, and she tried to figure out how to open it without the car on. Still dazed, she looked out the window and up, trying to see the officer. She lifted her hands in a gesture trying to tell him she couldn't open the window.

"Ma'am? Can you open the door? Are you hurt?" The voice was definitely a woman. Oh thank you lord! Annie thought.

"I don't know. I think it's locked, wait," Annie slowly reached forward with her left hand and felt a sharp pain shoot up her arm as she unlocked the door. Leaning back, she grabbed her left arm with her right, holding it to stop the pain.

The door opened, and the light from the flashlight made her wince.

"You're hurt. I'll call for an ambulance, so I don't want you to move," the woman spoke softly to her, but when she called in the report on her radio her voice became stern and professional.

Annie closed her eyes once more, and leaned her head back. Her arm throbbed. She must have busted something. She wiggled her toes. Nope. Fine. She'd never been in an accident. Ever. Is this how her parents felt? No, they died on impact didn't they? That's what they were told. Maybe she was dead too. Maybe this was all a vision of some sort. No, pain was too real. And of course this was no accident. She knew that. Whoever had tried to sideswipe her did it intentionally. Her life was a disaster. And she needed Chris. Where was she? Was she close?

"Ma'am?"

Annie jumped a little, startled again. "Yes, sorry, I just needed to rest for a second."

"I understand. I'm Deputy Sue Cantoni, Lakeside County Sheriff's Department. Can you tell me your name?"

"Annie Porter"

"Good. Do you know where you are?"

"Ohio?" She asked hopefully.

"Good. Can you tell me what happened?"

Annie sighed and closed her eyes for a moment. She'd made it. "This is gonna sound crazy, but someone ran me off the road."

"Not so crazy. It happens more often than you think. Did you get a look at the other vehicle?"

"No. Too dark," she struggled to talk. It seemed she couldn't catch her breath. Hurt to talk. "They came up really close behind me," Annie paused. "I tried to speed up. So they wouldn't hit me."

The deputy nodded, "Go on, if you can."

"The next thing I knew they were right there next to me swerving towards me." Annie paused again.

"I had to get out of the way. That's all I could think of," her tone had suddenly shifted remembering the panic she'd felt. "They hit me… I veered off the road and well, here I am."

"OK. I can see that's enough for now. The ambulance will be here in a minute, and we'll get you fixed up." She began to turn away and Annie stopped her.

"Wait, please, you're not leaving are you?" She didn't know why, but Annie felt comforted by her presence. It calmed her.

"No, I'll stay right here. Is there someone we can call?"

"No," she replied a bit too quickly. "I mean, yeah, I guess I should."

"Were you headed somewhere in particular? Is someone waiting for you?"

Now or never, Annie thought. She didn't know how close to the cabin she was, but she was in the right county. And if so, they might know Chris. Know where he is. All she had to do was pretend she knew too.

"I was on my way to visit a friend at his cabin. Chris Gregory. I've got his phone number with me." She tried for a rueful smile. "It's in my phone, which," she glanced around, "which is here somewhere I'm sure. It was on the seat next to me, must have rolled on the floor somewhere."

Annie sensed her suspicion immediately. Did she know him?

"Is he expecting you?"

Yep. Suspicious all right. "Not exactly, but I'm sure he'd appreciate it if you called him?" Annie mentally crossed her fingers. What if he didn't appreciate the call. No. Impossible. If nothing else, he'd want to know if she were hurt, wouldn't he? Unless...no! She would not listen to that voice in her head. Luce's voice. "Maybe it's Chris?" she could hear the questioning. Uh uh. No way. Too late, anyway. Officer Cantoni looked thoughtful. The sun was up now, and she could see her face clearly. She was a big woman, older than Annie had expected. Her frazzled red hair and blue eyes were friendly. And the laugh lines around her eyes indicated a warmth that she was sure not many picked up on. She had the look of someone who could be really tough if need be.

"I'll see if we can locate him for you, I don't suppose you have his address?" Sue replied with a reassuring smile.

"Um, I think it's here somewhere?" Annie mumbled, stalling as she tried to lean across for her purse. Her face grimaced in pain, there was no need to pretend on that score.

"It's ok. Leave it. I'll look it up." Sue spoke gently. She wasn't sure about this woman, but it didn't hurt anything to give her the benefit of the doubt. She wasn't going to bolt anywhere in her condition. And Sue hadn't given any indication that she knew how to find the guy.

"Thanks," Annie replied softly, looking beyond the deputy's shoulder at the ambulance pulling up. She really was hurting. And she was suddenly drained. She just wanted to sleep. For a long time. Maybe if she closed her eyes and just let things happen. Yeah. Just let things happen. Maybe they'd find Chris. She was so drowsy she never even noticed the gentle hands lifting her from the car, laying her on the stretcher. The pain was far away now. Sleepy. A prick in her arm. Soft voices. Then blissfully, nothing.

######

Sue Cantoni watched her boss, Luke Branson, approach from his car. He'd just retired from the Cleveland PD when he was elected Sheriff. He'd grown up here as she had. And both knew Chris Gregory well. He'd been coming here since he was just a kid with his dad, and had built his cabin just a few years back. Sue wasn't sure about this woman, but if Chris knew her, they better find out now. They'd had a few run-ins with overzealous McLain fans over the years. Fans who had somehow figured out his identity. They'd managed every time to thwart their efforts and convince them he wasn't their guy. Even the paparazzi. It had been at least a year since the last incident. But this was far more serious. If she was looking for Chris, or worse, he was expecting her, and someone had run her off the road… Sue frowned. When Chris had returned a few weeks ago he'd mentioned some trouble in New York. Asked them to be on the lookout for anything suspicious. This certainly fit the bill.

"Luke. We've got trouble."

"Fill me in."

Sue gave him a brief run down, and then waited for his reaction. He wasn't a hair-trigger response kind of guy. In his fifties, he was still tall, fit and youthful looking. The slight gray streaks in his thick blond hair just made him more distinguished. And he was cautious. Always. Right now he looked concerned, and his eyes crinkled in thought.

"Get a hold of him. Don't spook him. Don't mention the accident yet. Get his reaction to this woman asking for him first. Then we'll go from there. If you think he needs to know, tell him. You know him well, Sue, you make the call."

"OK. I'll try to call first, as I want to head over to the hospital and talk some more with her. I have a feeling she needs company anyway. She's frightened, that's for sure."

"Keep me posted" Luke replied with authority. Chris hadn't gone into detail about the incident in New York but Luke sensed real trouble around the bend. There was a part of him that dreaded it, though admittedly there was another that welcomed the rush of adrenaline and the purpose it gave him. He was after all, a cop.

Chapter 13

Annie opened her eyes, finding it difficult. Groggy. She was so groggy. Dark. Where was she? She tried to think.

She felt a light touch on her hand.

"Ms. Porter?" the voice was soft, familiar.

"Hmm?" Annie's mouth didn't seem to work. It was dry. Pasty.

"Here," said the voice again, and she felt a straw at her lips.

"Sip it. Slowly." Water. It felt good. She took a breath and tried to focus. Opened her eyes again. Let them adjust, she thought. Still dark. She couldn't see.

She tried to sit up, frantic. "I can't see. I cannot see!" she yelled turning her head towards the voice.

"Shhhh. It's ok. There's a bandage over your eyes. That's all. You're in the hospital, Annie. Do you remember? You've had an accident."

Annie laid her head back down and closed her eyes. Think. Think. Flashes. Lights. A car coming at her on the side.

"Yes," she murmured softly. "OK. I'm OK. I remember. I remember your voice. But I can't seem to get it straight."

"That's OK. I'm Sue Cantoni. I'm with the Sheriff's department." Sue looked down at Annie. She looked pale, and small. She was petite to begin with; she'd noticed at the scene. But now she looked almost childlike. Her brown hair swept back away from the injury over her eyes that had required the bandage. Her face was pale, and frightened. She had to ask questions, and it would be difficult. They hadn't found Chris. She'd called, but his voice mail was full. Then swung by his cabin. He was nowhere to be found. His SUV wasn't in the driveway. Hopefully he hadn't left town. Luke had put the other guys on alert if they spotted him. If he was in the area, they'd find him.

"Look, Annie, I hate to do this, but I've got some questions. I know you're feeling bad, and I promise to be brief. But I really want to get to the bottom of this all right?"

Annie sighed. "I know. But more than likely it was some drunk, right?"

"Could be. Or not. They've towed your car and are analyzing some of the paint scratches. It'll help identify the vehicle. But it takes a while. Is there anything else you can tell me that might help?"

Annie pursed her lips and then released a breath. "I think I was followed. No. I know I was. I thought it was me being paranoid. You know, driving in the early hours on a long dark highway kind of thing. But I think it was the same car all along."

"How long was someone tailing you?"

"Good lord, I don't know. I first noticed somewhere in the middle of Pennsylvania I think."

"Where were you coming from, New York? You have New York rental plates on the car."

"Yeah. I left the city around 11 last night."

Sue said softly, "So Monday night, correct?"

"Right. Wasn't yesterday Monday?"

"Yeah, but you've been out for a while, so I'm just checking."

"Oh," Annie barely got the word out.

"Chris? Did you call Chris?" Annie blurted it out without thinking.

"I'm sorry. We haven't located Chris Gregory yet." Sue hoped that would suffice for an answer.

"Can we call someone else?"

"Of course!"

Annie wished she could see the deputy's face. She needed to know if she could count on her. Then again, she had no choice now. Luce would know she'd left, probably thought she'd been murdered or kidnapped, and called Holman, who'd be annoyed as hell. She'd have to face the music sometime. But calling Luce directly was out of the question. When their parents died, Luce was the one to get the call. Annie would never, ever do that to her again.

"Do you know where my purse is?"

"Sure, it's right here," Sue grabbed it from atop the built-in dresser.

"If you look in the side zipper there's a business card," her voice was faltering. The drugs were kicking in again, she assumed. Once she realized the IV in her arm was dispensing something other than just fluids, she began to appreciate the tell-tale signs of pain relief. And oblivion…which was where she was headed again. "Call him. He can, can…" Annie lost her train of thought as she drifted once more into sleep.

Sue located the card and gave a small shake of her head. She should have known somehow this was all tied in with Chris and his "trouble" in New York. The card was for an NYPD detective. At least maybe now they'd get some answers, at least until they found Chris.

Andy paced back and forth behind his desk. He was one of the lucky ones. He actually had an 'office' or what served as one. The former broom closet, he was pretty sure. He turned and looked at the worried faces of those crammed in the small space with him. The Stoltz's were standing by the door, tightly squeezed together, more for comfort he thought than by necessity. They were truly worried, his gut wasn't steering him wrong. Then there was Mark Simeon, who'd brought his wife along, and they too, looked anxious as hell. Luce was sitting in the only chair, *his* chair, which she'd commandeered the minute she had stormed into his office demanding to know what he'd done with her sister. The woman had such an imagination, he thought as he studied her. So suspicious she thought he'd actually put her in hiding without telling her. And all because of a break-in at her apartment. Sure it was serious, and there was a threat involved, but witness protection wasn't offered to victims of burglaries. At least not in New York. But Luce was more than just nervous, she was scared. At least that's how Andy interpreted the fact that she was actually gnawing on her fingernails and her clothes were rumpled. Her dark straight hair was swept back in a clip, in a fairly haphazard way. So unlike the chic, always together Luce he'd come to know.

No one spoke. The tension was getting to all of them. Andy checked his watch, and looked over at Mark.

"You said Gregory would be here this afternoon? Did he give a time?"

Mark sighed. "Nope, just said he'd be on the next plane, then hung up."

"Does he know where to reach you?"

"Sure, he's got my cell number and said he'd call when he lands at LaGuardia."

"OK, then, Luce? I need you to think really hard. I know we've been through this a few times already, but, if Annie took off voluntary, where would she go?"

Luce glared at Andy. "If I knew that, we wouldn't all be sitting here. I'm telling you, something's happened. She wouldn't just take off. Can't you put out an APB or something?"

"We've been over this already. She can't be declared missing for 24 hours. There's no sign of foul play." Andy glared back, his frustration mounting. His gut told him Annie was in trouble, somehow, but he was powerless to act.

"But you told her to stay in town, remember? If, as *you* say, she left on her own, then she violated your orders, right? So you go have her picked up for that."

"This isn't a police state, Luce…" Andy abruptly turned as his intercom buzzed.

"Call on line 4, Detective, some Sheriff's deputy in Ohio." The voice crackled through.

Andy grabbed the phone and pushed the button to connect.

"Holman here"

"Detective Holman? Sue Cantoni, Lakeside County Ohio Sheriff's Office. I'm calling regarding Annie Porter."

Andy glanced up at the expectant faces in the room and nodded a confirmation that this was related to Annie.

"Go on," Andy spoke hurriedly into the phone.

"Well, I'm not sure what all this is about," Sue spoke hesitantly, "but she asked me to call you. Said you could help fill us in. I should tell you she's in County Hospital, a car accident."

"Hang on a moment, would you?" Andy turned to Luce. "Could I ask you and the others to wait outside please?" He didn't want them to overhear this, especially Luce. Especially if it was bad. God he hoped it wasn't.

Luce bit back a retort, knowing now was not the time to argue.

"OK, come on you guys, let's take it outside. Give the Detective here some privacy." Though her tone was slightly miffed, she knew she had no choice.

Andy waited till they'd all gone into the hall, and began speaking quietly to the deputy.

He asked first for Annie's condition. Satisfied that she was going to be OK, he began asking for details. They spoke for over a half an hour, each providing as much information as they could. It was a game of fill in the blanks. And by the time they'd finished, both the deputy and the detective had a fairly complete picture of what had happened. Right now, Chris

Gregory was the only missing link, and knowing that he was well known by the Sheriff and his team made him a bit surer that he wasn't involved, at least not in a criminal way. As soon as he arrived, they'd know more.

Whoever was behind this was deadly serious about it. He and the deputy both agreed on that. And with what she had related about Chris and what she knew of his personal life, Andy was beginning to narrow down the list. Passion, jealousy, it was evident that someone was trying to keep Annie and Chris from ever being together.

The whole thing was beginning to gel. He and Chris were going to have a talk. A long one. Because Chris's memories held the key. Annie's too. She was in no condition to be interrogated just yet, but the doctor attending her said she wouldn't be released for several days, which bought them some time. Now the question was what to tell Chris, and how to keep him from hopping the next plane back. If he was right about the perp, that would endanger them both.

Turning his thoughts back to his immediate problem, he took a deep breath. Telling Luce about this was not going to be easy. He had a hunch she was operating solely on adrenaline at this point.

She'd awoken to a noise at around 3am. Got up to grab a drink of water, found Annie gone and immediately called him. As much as he disliked being woken up in the middle of the night, the panicked sound of Luce's voice when she'd called kept his temper in check and put him on high alert. He'd managed to calm her down, but knew she hadn't gone back to sleep and probably wouldn't until Annie was found.

By now Luce was totally stressed, and combined with the lack of sleep, she wasn't going to take the news well.

Picking up his phone, he made a series of calls, and then gathered his thoughts. He'd have to tread carefully with Luce.

Opening his office door, he glanced across the hall. Luce was sitting on the floor, knees tucked under her, leaning her head back against the wall. Her eyes closed, she looked, well almost serene. A jolt of something went through him. An unidentifiable emotion. Certainly not something he was used to.

Was she asleep?

"Luce?" he spoke softly, unsure whether she'd respond.

She opened her eyes instantly, throwing her head forward in the process.

Without thinking, Andy automatically reached his hand out, intending to help her up. They both felt the surge when he grabbed her hand. And it left them both stunned. But only for a moment. They both regrouped quickly.

"What happened?" Luce demanded as she smoothed out her blouse and fidgeted with her hair.

"Come in for a moment," he said quietly as he led her into his office.

"Sit."

Luce looked at him curiously but did as he said.

"We've found Annie," he said in the same quiet voice he'd used in the hall. It was his cop training. The voice modulation they'd learned in training came in handy.

"Where is she? What's happened?" Luce's voice was anxious and her eyes were wide with fear.

"She's OK, Luce, but she's been in a car accident."

"That can't be. She left her car here, remember? Whose car? Where?" Luce was panicked now, her eyes darting back and forth from Andy to the doorway.

"Slow down, Luce, and I'll explain it all. OK?"

Luce tried to stop the shaking that had seemed to take control of her. She couldn't speak, so she just nodded.

Andy went on to explain what he knew. As soon as he got to the details of the accident, he watched her closely. Luce was reaching the breaking point and for some reason, his normal detachment disappeared. As the tears began welling in her eyes, he broke every rule he had. He pulled her up out of the chair, sat down himself, and pulled her onto his lap. She was trembling uncontrollably. Wrapping his arms around her, he began to smooth her hair back, and murmur. "Shh. Go ahead, cry. You'll feel better. Then I'll tell you the rest."

Nodding, Luce continued to let the tears fall, not even attempting to wipe them away. Her baby sister. Hurt and alone somewhere, with nobody beside her. Someone was trying to hurt her and Luce couldn't stop it. She was supposed to protect Annie. It was her job. And she was failing. And worse, she was nothing more than a simpering weak crybaby. But just for once, having someone strong to lean on felt good. Too good. It couldn't hurt to let go for just a few moments. And when those moments were over, she'd take control again. She had to.

Lifting her head, she fought back the urge to stay in the comfort of Andy's arms.

She gently pulled away and stood up. "I'm ok. Tell me the rest." Though her voice was back in control, she had turned her head away. Couldn't let him see how emotionally wrought she was.

Andy sensed the change and knew better than to challenge her.

He finished explaining what he knew, and waited for her expected response.

"I have to go to her. Now."

Andy smiled knowingly. He knew that's what she'd say. And he was ready.

"I know. Before I told you I went ahead and booked you a flight. You'll have to fly into Hopkins in Cleveland, and someone from the Sheriff's department will meet you there."

"I can rent a car. I don't need them to come get me."

"Yes, you do. Sometimes we all need things, Luce. It's not a bad thing. And you need the protection."

"Me?" she looked at him in surprise. "I'm not the one being stalked here, Annie is."

"We don't know that. Now. They'll meet your flight and that's the end of it." Andy reached over to the desk and handed her a slip of paper. "Here's the itinerary and flight information, it's an e-ticket, and you can get your boarding pass at the kiosk at LaGuardia. I've got a car waiting downstairs. He'll take you by your apartment on the way, so you can pick up some clothes."

Luce narrowed her eyes. "You planned all of this out for me? Who bought the ticket? Where did you get a car and driver?" Her tone was demanding. She knew she was being ridiculous. But she was inquisitive by nature and a pure control freak to boot. He'd completely taken over here, and that didn't sit well in her current state of panic.

Andy half grinned, enjoying her discomfort. At least it took her mind off Annie for a minute.

"No time to explain, Luce, you've got to get going if you're going to catch that flight." He ushered her out into the hall and pointed her towards the stairs. "Go," he said with a touch of humor as he gave her a little push. She took one last glance behind her, and whipped her head back around as she strode towards the stairs. He was really really unnerving her. And what kind of cop would do what he just did. Instinctively, she knew he'd paid for all this himself. The ticket, the car and driver. She glanced at the paper he'd handed to her, yep, hotel too. What kind of NYPD Cop could afford that? She'd pay him back of course, because it probably cost him the next two months' rent. But why did he do it? She thought about it all the way home. And on the way to the airport. And in the plane. But no answers came.

Chapter 14

Andy looked up when he heard the light knock.

"Come in," he called brusquely, knowing who it was and setting the tone from the get-go.

Mark entered first, followed by Chris, who looked like hell. Andy hadn't told anyone other than Luce about Annie, as he needed to once again eliminate suspects. And he'd hustled Luce out of the building before she could tell anyone else. Whether or not she just went ahead and sent them all a text, he couldn't know for sure, but he hoped he could trust her. He hoped she understood just how dangerous it would be. Bill and Jen had left when Mark headed to the airport to pick up Chris, and Mark's wife was waiting in the lounge down the hall. Andy was still debating whether to speak to these guys alone, or together. Maybe alone would be best.

"Mark, Chris," He nodded to each.

"Any word," Chris asked quickly, his face tense.

"Actually, yes, but I'd like to speak with Mark for a moment, if that's OK. Maybe you could give us a minute?"

Chris looked like he was going to argue, but thought better of it. "Fine, a minute, but I need to know she's OK."

"She's OK, Chris," Andy replied, tilting his head toward the door. "A minute, please?"

It wasn't a question, and Chris took the hint, though he didn't appear happy to comply.

As soon as he'd left, Andy looked pointedly at Mark.

"We've located her, Mark. In Ohio."

"Ohio," Mark replied nodding. "She went looking for Chris."

"Exactly." He went on and relayed much of what happened, careful not to reveal too much. He watched Mark's reaction carefully. Looking for clues. What did Mark know, and what would could he offer that might help?

Mark was forthcoming and thankfully, knew plenty. The detective was able to confirm much of what the sheriff's department had provided, and Mark seemed candid about it. Nothing was being hidden. Good sign. He could now interview Chris, and see how well everything meshed. One false move on Chris's part, and he'd know which direction to head. Since Chris had obviously taken a fairly early flight out that morning, odds were he couldn't have been involved at all.

"Chris, sit down," Andy said, keeping his tone even. Chris was wound pretty tight and Andy knew, assuming he wasn't behind Annie's problems, he'd probably go nuts when he heard the latest.

Chris sat quickly, and leaned forward, looking him directly in the eye.

"Where's Annie, Detective?"

"Sorry, Chris. I've got to ask a few questions first. You understand?"

"No, I don't. But go ahead. Get it over with."

"Where were you this morning, say between 5am and 8am?"

"At my cabin till about 5am. That's when Mark called and said Annie was gone."

"Then what?"

"I drove like a madman to the airport and hopped the next available flight and here I am."

"Do you have a copy of your boarding pass?"

Chris reached into his back pocket and pulled out the stub from the boarding pass and handed it to Andy, his eyes never leaving his face.

Andy scanned it, verifying the time and date. They'd already checked the passenger lists but booking a flight and being on it were two different things.

He was well on his way when Annie was run off the road.

"OK. I want you to listen, and try to stay calm a moment. Can you do that?"

Chris nodded; his knuckles white as he clenched his fists.

Andy took a breath, and then recited precisely what he'd told Mark and Luce. He watched Chris carefully, taking note of his reaction. Calm at first, then he could see the muscles in his face twitch. With careful deliberation, Chris stood up.

"I'm going, Detective, and there is no way in hell you can stop me. You know, if you hadn't stopped us from seeing each other, she wouldn't have been on that road. This wouldn't have happened." He turned toward the door, and Andy quickly got up and maneuvered around the desk, reaching him at the door. Laying a firm hand on his shoulder, he spoke softly.

"Chris, if you go, you'll only put her in more danger. Do you understand?" Chris paused, and slowly lowered his head. He knew the detective was right. But his gut was being wrenched and his only thoughts were of Annie, lying in a hospital, hurt, scared, lonely.

"We're going to figure this out Chris. I promise. In the meantime, there are good people looking out for her. Luce is on her way there as well. They're taking great care of her."

He went on and explained the call from the Sheriff's department, and who was with Annie. It seemed to calm him somewhat.

Chris sat back down, and tried to regroup.

"Can I call her?" he sounded so hopeful Andy winced.

"No Chris, no contact for now. It's safer this way."

"Will you at least send her a message for me? I need you tell her I'm still here OK? Trust me she needs to know. Tell her we are still on for that date, OK? Please?"

"OK. I can do that much." He gave Chris a sympathetic smile. They continued talking for over an hour, and Chris was beginning to show some strain.

"Detective," Chris interrupted at one point. "What could any of this have to do with Annie? I don't get it. I wrote a book. Just a book." All this talk about his past, Annie's past, it made no sense. *Why would anyone hurt Annie?*

"That's what we're trying to determine, Chris. I know this is tough, I know you'd rather be with her right now, but if we're going to protect her, we've got to dig deep here. Are you still with me?"

Chris nodded and sighed. "Yeah, go on, let's finish this up."

"First, you said just now it's just a book. Is it?"

"What do you mean?"

"Is it just a book, or is it personal? Are the characters completely fictional, or based on real people?"

"Ok, I get it. It's not just a book. They're real."

"As I thought. Now tell me about Sam, Chris. You guys go way back, right?"

"Since we were kids. We grew up down the street from each other."

"And you roomed with him in school?"

"Sure. We were inseparable for the most part. Till Martha."

"His girlfriend?"

"Yeah, she was okay, you know? Except a little wild…drinking, experimenting with drugs. That kind of thing."

"How about Sam? Was he into it as well?"

"No, and it ticked him off. In fact, they broke up for a while, went through a rough period. He wanted her to mellow out, she wouldn't."

"But they got back together?"

"Eventually, but not before he'd screwed up pretty bad. She caught him in bed with another girl. Not a pretty thing." Chris grimaced as he recalled the scene. "It got really nasty. Martha wouldn't talk to Sam for a few weeks.

Finally, they seemed to get back on track. Martha cooled it on the drugs, and everything seemed to be fine. Apparently we were all fooled. She was back on the drugs and, well, as you recall, she OD'd."

"Who was the girl Sam slept with?"

Chris shook his head. "Nora," he said dryly.

"Nympho Nora?" Andy asked curiously.

"So you've heard that, huh? Must have been Annie." Chris shook his head, a small smile upon his face. For the first time Andy began to see an emotion in Chris that went beyond being angry or nervous. This perhaps was the real Chris Gregory.

"Yes, I take it there's no love lost there."

"Hardly!"

"So Sam and Annie, did they get along?"

"Sure. I always figured Annie and him, well, if it weren't for Martha, I would have thought they'd have hooked up." Chris looked resigned.

Andy narrowed his eyes. "Sam and Annie? Why did you think that?"

Andy couldn't help but wonder if Chris was a dense as he appeared to be.

"I don't know, they just seemed to like each other. She was always stopping in to see him."

"And not you?"

"No. I hoped for a while, until Sam told me flat out that it was him she wanted."

Andy sat back, hands clasped behind his head.

"Did they ever date?" Curious now, Andy wanted to push a few buttons. See what they would lead to.

Chris bristled a bit. "Nah, Sam tried to put the moves on her once at a party, Martha was there, but out of it. Annie turned him down flat. Said he already had a girlfriend. Annie would never poach."

"And after Martha died?"

"I heard he did try again, but Annie said she wouldn't date someone on the rebound from something so horrendous."

"So she shot him down twice?" Andy was honing in now. As much to complete the picture as to get Chris to wake up and realize his mistake.

"I guess. And you know, the thing is he didn't even seem to care." Chris bit off the last part of that, looking annoyed now.

"Look, you're tired, I'm hungry. Let's take a break, eh?"

"And do what detective? I can't go home, I can't see Annie. What is it you expect me to do while you figure it all out?"

#######

"Ouch!" Annie cried as she winced.

"Hold still, Ms. Porter, it'll be over in a moment."

The voice was deep, male and reassuring, Annie thought, and if his looks matched his voice, he'd be one sought after doctor. As long as you didn't require treatment. Gentle he wasn't. That was the third time he'd yanked her hair out with the adhesive on the bandage.

"Look, Dr. Grange, I like my hair. I like it where it is. On my head," she gritted her teeth as again she felt that yanking sensation.

The doctor chuckled. "Almost there, kid, almost there."

Kid. Hmmph, Annie thought. I'll bet he's fresh out of school himself.

She blinked as she felt the weight of the last of the bandage removed. The light was blinding at first and she quickly shaded her eyes with her hand. No easy feat with the IV tugging at her wrist. She turned to look up at the tall shadow by the bed. As her eyes focused, she noted he was a pretty good specimen. Not bad for the first thing she'd laid eyes on in days. She managed a weak smile.

"Torture session all through doc?" she inquired, not quite politely. Good looking he may be, but her scalp still smarted from his ministrations.

"All through," he smiled broadly. "I'll come back later and we'll see if we can't get you up and around."

"That would be nice," Annie sighed. "I'm not used to just lying around being waited on. Though it does have its merits." She laughed softly, then winced. It hurt to laugh.

"It's the ribs. They're bruised, and you'll find coughing, laughing and sudden movement will be uncomfortable, at least for another few days. So try and stay as relaxed as you can. If it gets bad, go ahead and push the button on this," he said as he handed her a small unit that looked like a game controller. "It will dispense a controlled dose of pain medication which should ease things a bit. Make you more comfortable."

"You could have told me about this before," Annie grumbled.

Dr. Grange laughed again. "I could have, but we'd been administering your meds through the IV until you were capable of managing it yourself!"

"Well I'm capable now," Annie replied as she looked around her. Not too bad for a community hospital, she thought. She'd expected a stark, efficient looking room, all chrome and linoleum, but was surprised at the hominess she saw. The walls were painted in pastels, with scalloped edge curtains over the window. Several paintings hung on the walls. Originals not prints, showing variations of a lakefront scene. The linens were white, but everything else in the room had color. It was soothing, and Annie somehow felt comforted by it.

"Nice place here, doc," Annie quipped. "But I don't think I want to stick around much longer, when can I get out of here?"

"Hey what's this? You just got here and already you're ready to flee? What, have we offended you? Don't like our company?" He laughed, a full rich sound that made Annie smile. "It's going to be at least a few days. Then we'll see. We need to get those ribs healed, and you're pretty banged up. Soon, though…" his voice trailed off as he disappeared out the door with a brief wave.

Annie grinned to herself. Yep, cute. But she had bigger fish to fry, and no little accident was going to stop her. She stopped grinning suddenly remembering that more than likely it was no accident.

Chapter 15

The diner was busy, it always was, the strong smells of coffee and grease permeating everything. Somehow Andy knew he'd find them all here. Location is everything, and this one was right next to the precinct. The atmosphere was perfect for what he had in mind. A nice casual conversation where everyone felt relaxed enough to say whatever came into their heads. Sometimes it was the best strategy. Put them totally at ease and see what happens. Though he didn't think Chris could relax under any circumstance, it was worth a shot.

"Mind if I join you?" Andy posed the question, and then sat without waiting for a reply, forcing Mark, Julie, Jen, Bill and Chris to slide over inside the large circular booth.

"Why no, please do," Chris muttered.

"The usual, Karen," Andy looked up as their server came over. Obviously a regular, Chris thought. He wasn't happy with this guy. Keeping Chris from Annie seemed pretty cruel and unwarranted. And he needed someone to direct his anger and frustration on. This cop seemed as good a target as any.

Once the food arrived, the conversation ceased for a bit. Andy waited for just the right moment.

"I read your book, you know," Andy began without looking at Chris for a response.

Andy put his cheeseburger down, and wiped his fingers carefully on a napkin, deliberately stalling. "Your book's victim, Gwen, right? Correct me if I'm wrong, but just working through all this, Gwen I'm guessing is based really loosely, on Martha," Andy went on without waiting for a response. "Which says to me that maybe you don't think Martha's death was an accidental overdose, or a suicide for that matter. Maybe deep down you think someone killed her."

"To be honest, I guess there was always a doubt in my mind," Chris acknowledged grudgingly.

"Just thinking out loud here, but," Andy paused as if in thought, "is it possible that someone thinks Annie knows what happened? After all, in the book, your reporter character, Jade, is based on Annie, right? And Jade suspects something."

"That's nuts!" Chris blurted out. "I'm the one who wrote the book so I would be the one who knows what happened."

"But Chris, nobody knows you wrote the book, right? So you'd have to agree it's possible someone thinks Annie wrote the book."

"I hadn't thought about that."

"Who's Martha?" Julie interrupted, suddenly very interested.

"Sam's girlfriend back in college," Chris replied.

"Oh, good, I thought maybe she was yours," Julie looked relieved. Chris shot her a look that clearly said she was mistaken.

"OK," Andy began again. "Hear me out. Let's just say, for arguments sake, that someone wanted Martha out of the way all those years ago. Who's the most likely suspect?" No one said anything for a moment.

"The boyfriend?" Jen spoke up this time, her attention wholly captured.

"Maybe," said Andy. "Now, motive?"

"She dumped him?" Julie instinctively replied.

"Not likely," Chris jumped in. "She worshipped him. If anything, he tried to dump her and couldn't." He frowned as he realized what he'd said. "Not that Sam would ever have done anything like that. No, he wouldn't have."

"You did say he wanted to date Annie, Chris, and that she refused because of Martha."

"Yeah but it's a huge leap from wanting to date someone to murder!"

"I don't know, Chris," Mark jumped in. "It depends on how Sam really felt about Annie. Think about it. Wasn't it Sam who told you Annie wasn't interested in you? And if he wanted Annie badly enough, and thought Martha was in the way…"

"This is absurd," Chris said loudly. "Sam and I have known each other practically our whole lives. You want me to believe he wanted Annie so badly he'd murder for her? Remember I told you he didn't actually give a damn that she turned him down?" Chris shook his head, realization dawning.

Andy decided to change direction. "Who knows about your cabin, Chris?"

"You mean does Sam know, don't you? Yeah, he helped build it."

"So he'd know the area pretty well, then?"

"I suppose. Look, this is crazy. You want me to believe Sam ran Annie off the road? No way. And whoever did was following her for a while, right? So they're not necessarily from around the lake area. Look, you can speak to Sam yourself. You'll see. He's just not the type."

"Care to test the theory?" Andy looked around the table.

No one spoke up, so Andy continued. "The closer Annie gets to you, the more desperate they appear to be. So let's make whoever it is think you're together. I'll set it up to appear you and Annie are headed to the cabin. We'll see who turns up."

"You want to use Annie as bait? Uh uh. Not a chance," Chris responded adamantly.

"Annie won't be in any danger, I promise. Neither will you. It's the only way. If in fact it is your buddy Sam, we'll know soon enough. If not, we'll know that too."

###

Annie looked down at the tray of food and frowned. She'd heard hospital food was bad, but this was ridiculous. There was the main plate, with some sort of unidentifiable meat surrounded by lumpy grayish white stuff she assumed was potatoes. There were some green beans, though they were a brownish color now, and just a tad shriveled. The cup of applesauce didn't look too bad, but she'd kill for a cheeseburger right about now.

"Looks like I'm just in time!"

Annie looked up in surprise, and smiled when she saw Luce in the doorway. She looked a bit frazzled, but Annie was more concerned with the takeout bag she was holding. The smell reached her immediately, causing her stomach to growl.

"Tell me that's a cheeseburger and I'll owe you forever, sis," Annie called out.

Luce grinned as the relief washed over her. Annie was ok. That's all that mattered.

"Yep, with everything. The guy who brought me here from the airport wasn't too thrilled about the detour, but, hey, nothing's too good for my sister!" Luce laughed and strode over to the bed. Seeing the tubes suddenly sobered her, but she quickly recovered. She knew better than to let Annie see her distressed.

Luce grabbed the plate of questionable food from Annie's tray, and replaced it with the takeout burger and fries. Pulling up the chair by the wall, she sat down next to the bed and took Annie's hand.

"You're ok?" she asked softly.

"Yeah, I'll be fine. At least that's what my doctor the hunk says."

"Hunk?" Luce asked innocently, though Annie could see the wheels churning in her head. Nothing tempted Luce more than a smart, rich, guy and doctors were always on her A list.

"Yep, hunk. You'll see. So I'm guessing word's out on my adventure?"

"Yeah, big time. You'll have to fill me in on most of it. All I know is I got up in the middle of the night and you were gone. I freaked, called Andy, I mean Detective Holman. You remember him, don't you?"

"No brain damage, Luce, my memory is intact."

"Good. That's a relief. Anyway, I demanded he find you, which I have to say he wasn't all that cooperative about it. That man can be so bullheaded. Typical cop."

Annie smiled at her sister, knowing that there was more here between those two. Wisely, she said nothing.

"So I guess at some point you must have had someone call him. The next thing I know I'm here! Very weird, sis, he arranged everything. Down to the plane ticket. Not that I don't appreciate it, but it was a bit on the bizarre side."

"Hey. At least you're here. Now, enough about you. I'll tell you what happened, but only if you agree to help me."

"Help you what?"

"See Chris."

"Uh uh, no way. Is that what you were up to? He's not even here, you know. He's in New York. He was on his way there when Andy shipped me off. Didn't even let me hang around long enough to see the guy!"

"He's in New York? That figures. I drove 500 freaking miles, got run off the road, all for nothing."

"Actually, he was either here, or somewhere else, but when he heard you were missing, he hopped the next plane."

"How did he know I was gone?" Annie was surprised.

Luce grinned slyly, "Well, as soon as I hung up with Andy, I mean the detective, I called Jen, who called Mark, who called Chris."

Annie looked away for a moment, a smile on her face. He must care about me, she thought with satisfaction. Well, that's a start. She stiffened suddenly, and looked at Luce wide eyed. "He knows, doesn't he. That I drove out here. In fact everyone knows. I'm going to have to go into hiding now. This is too embarrassing, even for me!" her voice was panicky.

"I don't know what he knows, Annie, but don't worry about it now. It's small potatoes compared to the trouble you've been in. Someone's trying to hurt you if you recall, and whether or not Chris knows about this crush of yours is pretty unimportant at this point. Now spill it!"

Annie sighed, resigning herself to the fact that her deepest secrets, her unrequited love, was now common knowledge. "OK. Long story short, Luce, here it is. I was trying to figure out where Chris could be, and I remembered how often he spoke of someday building a place on this lake. He told me at the party he'd finally built his cabin. So, I figured I'd come here and find him. Rented a car and just took off."

"Well that worked out well."

"Maybe not, but I waited half my life for a legit date with Chris, and then when I'm finally going to get it, all this happens. So forgive me if I decided to take things into my own hands for once."

A light tap at the door caught their attention.

"Can I come in?" Sue Cantoni smiled as she entered, not waiting for an answer.

"I guess since you're here," Annie said, sighing for effect. She really did like Sue. And she'd been sticking close by her through this.

"I just got off the phone with Detective Holman. Are you up for a few more questions?"

"Of course."

"First I have a message for you. Your date is still on," Sue smiled as she said it. Sometimes being the bearer of good news could really outweigh the bad.

Annie actually grinned hearing that. "As if I'd let him back out now!"

"OK, now, I'll try to keep this short, ok? And please don't jump to any conclusions," Sue cautioned, then looked over at Luce. She knew it was Annie's sister, as she'd given clearance for her to visit.

Luce reached out one arm and smiled.

"Luce Porter, nice to meet you. You're the one who found her, right?"

"Yes, good to meet you Luce, I'm Deputy Sue Cantoni."

"Well I really want to thank you. You saved her life I'm sure and I can see you've taken good care of her. I really appreciate it. It's just us, you know. Our parents are gone. So, well, anyway, thanks." Luce wasn't big on being grateful or expressing it for that matter. But this woman had taken care of Annie when she couldn't, and it just seemed a bit humbling.

"I'm so sorry to hear that," Sue responded gently. There was obviously more to this story but now just wasn't the time.

"OK," Annie broke in. "Fire away with those questions before I hit the panic button again!" Annie looked at her medicine dispenser unit wistfully, then settled back into the stack of pillows behind her, trying to get comfortable. She was still sore, especially in her ribs, and even the meds did nothing more than take the edge off the pain. She suspected they'd lowered the dose just a bit.

"OK. We think whatever is happening now is directly related to something that happened years ago, and of course, that book. Which is why I'm going to ask these questions. First, when was the last time you saw or spoke with Sam Peckett?"

"Sam?" Annie thought for a moment. "You don't think it's Sam do you?"

"No conclusions, remember?" Sue reminded her.

"Oops. Sorry. OK. Sam Peckett. Let's see, about 6 years ago maybe. I came back here for a wedding, and ran into him at a bar we'd all gone to after the reception. He was with Nora. I don't suppose you've heard of her. I spoke to them for maybe a few minutes then ran like hell out the door."

"Nora. I know a bit about her, what the detective shared."

"Well, not my favorite person. Which is why I didn't stand around and chat for too long." Annie shivered for emphasis. "She gives me the creeps."

Sue nodded. "OK. Let me ask you this. Sam's girlfriend, Martha. She OD'd, correct?"

"That's what they said. But somehow, I don't think so. Martha was pretty nuts, you know, wild, but she was also careful. She never took more than she could handle. It never made sense to me. I think the drugs were bad, is what I think." Annie thought for a moment. "They tried to say it was probably deliberate, but that's just not Martha. She never would have done it on purpose."

"Was Sam involved with anyone other than Martha?"

"If I'm not mistaken, and I rarely am," Annie said wryly, smiling as Luce made a face, "I'm guessing Sam and Nora were together more than a time or two. Nora would jump in bed with anything as long as it was breathing."

"Tell me more about Nora, if you're up to it. Whatever you can."

She shook her head as she silently remembered. They'd been friends once, Annie recalled. It all began at the most awkward time for any girl. 13. 13, and discovering all kinds of inconvenient things about her body. Her hormones. Feelings. That's just about the time she met Nora.

She sighed as she looked over at Sue.

"Nora was new in school, just moved to town. Super friendly if not a little loud. I met her at lunch one day and it was like we were instant friends. Or so I thought."

"With friends like that," Luce interrupted, but didn't finish her sentence.

Annie darted a look over at Luce, silently telling her to shut up please.

"We had sleepovers and on the weekends we'd go exploring in the woods or played campout in the basement. And we told each other our deepest darkest secrets. Which is how it all exploded."

Annie closed her eyes and grimaced as she thought back. "Danny. That was my secret."

Her big crush. Danny was a year older, and had a killer smile. Oh he wasn't the best-looking boy in school, or the smartest, or the most talented. But he was Annie's crush. And she told Nora in secrecy and Nora swore not to tell. Well, she kept her secret. But had one of her own.

"So, I told Nora I was crushing on Danny. And then came *the* weekend. Everybody was going to the waterpark. *Everybody*. Nora was meeting us there." Annie's frown grew.

"When we got there, Luce and I scoped out the sandy beach area for a good place to see and be seen and I found the perfect spot and grabbed Luce's arm. I remember being soooo excited, I was practically shouting. 'There, it's perfect! Quick let's grab it!' Or something like that," Annie added.

"So Luce began heading over there and suddenly she stops dead in her tracks and says 'No Annie, let's go over there,' and points in a completely different direction."

"I remember Annie was like why? Everyone is over there," Luce interrupted again. "So I just said 'trust me you don't want to go over there.'"

"I remember stopping and looking over at my perfect spot. It was horrifying. There was Nora, looking way too cozy with none other than Danny. Luce was the only other person in the world who knew about Danny. Of course looking back, Nora and Danny were probably just sitting a bit too close, but there was Nora laughing and giggling way too loud."

It had devastated Annie. "I'm sure you understand, this was violating the sacred oath of friendship. So things were never the same. I vowed I would NEVER be friends with Nora again. I wanted to give her a piece of my mind, but then she saw me."

Annie was getting upset just thinking about it, Sue could see that, but she needed to understand the dynamics.

"Go on, Annie, what happened then?"

"She starts yelling at me to come over there, she saved us a place and so on. There was nothing we could do but head over there and act like nothing had happened. It was torture. But I lived through it. In fact for the rest of the day, Nora stopped flirting with Danny and acted as if it had never happened. Trying to get *me* to sit by Danny and flirt. I was young and stupid, and by the end of the day figured her flirting with him was all my overactive imagination. But obviously it would happen again and again after that. So I learned to cope."

Cope, she thought to herself, yeah right. She avoided Nora when she could and never again told her any of her secrets. It was an odd relationship they had, Nora assuming they were friends, Annie knowing they truly weren't. The occasional movie or study night to keep the charade going. Never quite having the nerve to confront Nora as she should have. Maybe if she had, she thought, as she felt herself drifting off back to sleep.

"What about you? Did you ever go out with Sam?" Sue tried to bring Annie's attention back to the present. It's difficult interviewing a patient on pain meds. Sifting through what's now and then, their memories generally become pretty tangled up.

Annie snorted. "Not likely. First of all, he wasn't my type. Not at all. Secondly, I only had eyes for Chris, I guess that's no secret. Well, maybe it is to you, did our friend the detective fill you in on all this?" Annie cocked her head to the side, wondering just how much Sue knew.

"Yes, what he knows, I know. How's that?" Sue smiled warmly.

"So then maybe you could tell me if I wasted my time coming up here?"

"What do you mean?"

Annie chewed on her lip. When she spoke, her voice was almost pleading. "OK. Bottom line is Chris didn't know I was coming. I didn't know exactly where the cabin was either. And since you now know what's going on, I think it's only fair to tell me maybe, if you know, does he have someone? I mean he *is* single, right? I assume you know. This is like a small town, right?"

Sue laughed softly. "Fair enough question. I'm sure you realize that we need to protect his privacy. He's been coming up to the lake for years, and it's our job to see he lives in peace. Keep the crazed fans from stalking him."

Annie smiled sheepishly. "Yeah, and you'd be right, wouldn't you. I mean anyone who drives 500 miles in the middle of the night just to see a guy must be a little crazed."

"Hey, love will do that to you, and yes, for the record, quite single. But, back to Sam."

"Right. Sam," Annie continued, "Sam was dating Martha, who happened to be my friend. Unlike Nora, I don't sleep with my friends' boyfriends."

"What about after Martha died?"

"No, for all the same reasons. Ooooh!" Annie winced suddenly as pain shot through her ribcage. Her finger automatically hit the button as she closed her eyes and waited for the medicine to kick in again. No one spoke, as they could see her face contort in pain, then relax again.

"You OK?" asked Luce.

"Yeah, sorry, that was harsh."

Sue hesitated for a moment. "Just one or two more, okay?" she asked gently.

"Sure. I'm ready." Annie reply, gritting her teeth as the last spasms of pain dissipated.

"Did Sam try? Ask you out?"

"You know he actually did, once or twice, and I figured he was just lonely. He really wasn't interested in me. I knew that. But what's all this leading to? I can't really figure this out. Of course I'm a bit loopy from this pain stuff, but still..." her voice trailed off as her eyes drooped close. She opened them again with a start, trying to remain awake.

"Look, Annie, that's enough for now. I'll stop by tomorrow, and we'll visit some more."

Annie closed her eyes and nodded. "mmm hmm...ok...bye..." and was out like a light.

Chapter 16

Crouching down, Sue peered intently at the damage to the otherwise pristine exterior of the vehicle. "Luke? Wanna take a look?" Without moving from her crouched position at the front of the car, Sue reached into her bag and grabbed her camera and began photographing at a rapid-fire pace. Sheriff Branson came around the side of the car to examine the spot Sue was so intent on.

"Well," he hesitated for a minute. "This doesn't look good does it. Looks like we need to have a little chat with Sam."

The Sheriff paused before ringing the bell. He'd known Sam about as long as he'd known Chris. Those two had been inseparable as kids, coming up to the lake every summer with the Gregory family. Nice enough guy Luke thought to himself, but this wasn't looking good. Jealousy and resentment? Could be. Only one way to find out.

Sam's head was pounding and the incessant *riiiiinnnnng* sound was painful at best. Normally he'd think this is the price you pay for a night out but he hadn't gone anywhere last night. In fact he'd hit the sack early. Must be sick. Flu. Damn that ringing won't stop. He slowly got out of bed and stumbled, grabbing the floor lamp for balance. Whoa. Not good. The door. The door... get the door. Not sure how he knew it was the door making the noise but he blindly just headed towards it and yanked it open. And fell straight forward into Luke.

"Hey there, Sam, you ok?" Luke's reflexes were quick and his arms went out in front to steady what appeared to be a highly intoxicated Sam. Grabbing him in a bear hug he eased him down on to the front stoop and tried to keep him upright.

"Had a little too much fun last night Sam?" Luke kept the question friendly and jesting. Taking a few deep breaths, Sam began to shake his head slowly, then after a few more deep breaths lifted it up and stared directly at what appeared to be the Sheriff.

"Not a drop Sheriff, must be a virus or the flu or something. I. Ate…"

Lurching sideways he threw one hand in the air as he involuntarily heaved over the side rail.

Slowly he turned back. "Sorry," he slurred a bit. Wincing, he looked again at the Sheriff. "This isn't right. My head is exploding. I need…" his voice trailed off as he closed his eyes and lost consciousness.

Senses in high gear, Luke summoned the ambulance, and reinforcements for Sue. Something was way off here.

The ambulance arrived within minutes along with the fire truck. Standard procedure.

"Carbon Monoxide, Sheriff," one of the firefighters who'd accompanied the EMTs approached Luke quickly. "And looks like someone tampered with the detector too," he added.

"Thanks Mike, hang out a moment will you?" he responded as he made his way over to Sue. "You better head over to the hospital with this one, and keep an eye out."

After getting briefed, Sue quickly got in her patrol car and headed out behind the ambulance to follow them. It was all coming together and she was on high alert now. Not just one patient to watch out for, but two. And their entrapment plans? Not going to be necessary it seems.

As a precaution, a deputy was stationed outside Annie's door 24/7. Now of course they'd need one outside Sam's door as well. With a department as small as theirs, they would be stretching things thin. Luke knew however that whoever was behind all this wasn't finished yet. The good news, if there was any to be had, was they'd narrowed down their list of suspects. With the added help of the NYPD and some favors called in from the Cleveland PD, they had their target.

Annie slept soundly, giving Luce a chance to go get a bite and relax a bit. Her hotel was right next door, and thankfully a 24-hour diner as well. Though even with Annie under careful guard, she couldn't totally get rid of that nagging sensation that something was about to happen.

######

The officer nodded politely at the nurse as she approached Annie's room, glancing at her ID hanging on the lanyard around her neck. Flipped over. Holding a hand up to stop her, he smiled apologetically.

"I'm sorry, can I see your ID please?"

The nurse quickly flashed it and the officer waved her in.

Annie opened one eye, somehow she didn't feel ready to wake up, but something was off. That medicine she'd taken a little while ago seemed to be too potent. It was just some over the counter pain meds, she had thought. The two little pills in the cup. Groggy. Too groggy. Just a nurse, she thought, fiddling with her IV. Whatever. But it was dark. They don't do this stuff in the dark. Wake up, she thought. Wake up.

"What's that, what are you doing?" Annie spoke slowly, even though inside she was approaching panic mode she knew it was probably all in her head.

"Don't mind me, sweetie, just go back to sleep. Take a good long nap."

Nap. It's the middle of the night, she thought.

"Hey whatever it is I don't want it right now if you could just go." She raised her voice hoping to alert whoever was outside her door but it seemed to come out a whisper. What if they weren't there? What if they'd taken a coffee break? Something was soooo not right. Maybe she could just rip the IV out, no, too painful. It's all in my mind, she thought. No, it's not.

Suddenly the nurse came to the side of the bed and Annie could see her up close. No way. No way. Nora. How the hell could Nora be in her room. Nurse Nora.

Without even thinking, instinct took over.

As loud as she could, and with as much surprise as possible, she almost screamed at her.

"Nora?" Annie's voice a mixture of fear and disbelief. "Oh my god, Nora? Is that you?"

The returning smile from Nora was anything but that of an old friend. More like that of the wicked witch.

"Hello, Annie, what an unexpected surprise this is, no?"

Nora's voice was hushed. "Been far too long, hasn't it Annie. Haven't seen you since Ronnie's wedding. You remember, I was with Sam and you were there, oh wait, alone, that's right. You're always alone, aren't you Annie. I've made sure of that. I thought you were always after Sam of course," Nora's voice began to get louder. She was losing control.

"Because that's what you told me. Then I read the book. Funny, it was Sam's copy. I borrowed it. It was inscribed you know, by the author. It's all there isn't it Annie? It was always Chris wasn't it. Well, now I know. But you can't have him. You'll never have him." She was shouting now. "Say goodnight Annie."

Annie tried to sort through it all in her head, as she watched Nora turn and reach for the IV line. All Annie could do was hope that help was on the way as sleep overtook her once again.

The officer heard the suddenly raised voice of the nurse, and calling for back up burst into the room. Seeing her at the IV with a syringe in her hand, he approached, gun drawn, cautiously. "Put it down, and back away slowly."

"I've got to give her this medication officer, that's my job." Nora's voice was brusque, professional and totally unfazed by the gun.

"I'm sure you do. But right now, I need you to take three steps back and drop to your knees, hands behind your head. Now."

######

Annie smiled as Luce arrived bearing gifts. One last junk food meal before returning to reality. Because in reality, Luce would never be bringing her Bob's Midnight BBQ special! Only in a world so topsy turvy that she ends up being run off the road by a maniac trying to kill her out of some murderous rage. Was it Nora all along? And then there was the new reality of Chris. All this stuff surrounding a guy she still hadn't even had a legit date with yet. But, no time to dwell on life's most embarrassing moments right now, there's Barbecue to be eaten. Guilt free.

"Knock knock!" Sue's voice rang out cheerfully as she walked in. And the sight of Annie elbow deep in pulled pork and ribs made her laugh outright. Luce, ever the elegant one, seated next to the bed with a small salad and tea. What a contrast, she thought. "OK ladies, looks like we have some updates to share."

Somewhat reluctantly, Annie sighed, putting down the bit of heaven she was eating. "All ears, Sue, please, is it over now?" Annie's voice was hopeful. Though even if it was over, it wouldn't be over until that awkward and inevitable next meet up with Chris.

"Well, there is some news, and yes, I do believe it's over." Sue replied warmly. She gave them both a minute to digest what she was saying, then continued. "We were able to find the vehicle that ran you off the road, Annie" Sue went on. "It was Sam Peckett's."

Annie sat up straight as her eyes widened. "No way, Sam? Well call me gob smacked. Sam was in on it? Sam tried to kill me?" She let out her breath with a whoosh. "That son-of-a-bitch!"

"Not so fast, Annie," Sue cautioned her. "As I was saying, it was Sam's car. But Sam wasn't driving it. Nora Jacobs was."

"Wow. She really had it in for me, huh. She always was a lousy driver," Annie muttered that last part under breath. Luce smiled, the wise-cracks were a good sign that Annie was OK.

Sue tried to give a general run down on what they knew.

"Did you know Nora went on to nursing school?"

Annie shook her head in disbelief.

"Well, seems she also stuck around Sam on and off over the years but it never really went anywhere. From what we've learned, they'd hook up occasionally but no more than that. When Chris wrote his new book we think it somehow triggered Nora. She realized it was Chris you were pining after." Sue paused to gauge Annie's reaction.

Annie nodded. "I don't remember word for word what she said to me the other night, but that sounds about right. It's still all a bit fuzzy."

Luce however was nodding her head up and down furiously. "Of course Annie, that's it! Nora always wanted what you wanted!"

Slowly Annie shook her head. "It really is absurd, who'd want my life? But go on."

Sue took a breath, then continued. "When we realized it could be Sam's car, we went out to his house and took a look to verify. Lucky for Sam we did, as we found him barely conscious. Seems someone had left the gas on and the CM detector broken."

Annie gasped. "Sam? She tried to kill Sam?"

"Someone did," Sue replied. "Again, luckily, unsuccessfully." Sue paused, as if trying to determine how much should be shared. "The long and the short of it is that Nora Jacobs is in custody, and you, Annie, are safe and cleared to go home. The DA is requesting no bail, so there shouldn't be any issues. While we're certainly going to need to talk to you again, probably a few depositions in store, but for now, you could use a little time off from all this. Plus I think someone is really, really needing to see you right about now," Sue smiled as she winked at Annie.

The rest could wait she decided. As it turned out, Nora Jacobs was unfortunately not quite mentally stable, however, with an attorney present, they'd been able to question her for several hours. Ms. Jacobs had vacillated between being very open and honest and completely defiant. But that interview also provided them with reason to believe that she was behind the death of Sam's old girlfriend. It was all speculation at this point, and certainly not information that she could share with Annie.

Luce noticed Annie immediately start gnawing her lip. "Stop that!" Luce commanded her as any big sister would. "I brought you your clothes, so take one last bite of that garbage you call food and then get dressed. We are so out of here."

Annie didn't stop gnawing on her lip however, continuing to let her nerves get the best of her all the way back to New York. They landed at

LaGuardia, and as they grabbed their bags off the carousel, Luce stiffened. "What?" Annie cried out immediately thinking they were in danger again.

Plastering her best gracious smile, Luce turned toward the exit. "Detective. How nice."

"Ms. Porter," Andy replied with a nod and a smirk.

Annie rolled her eyes. "Listen up, you two, I've had a really hard week, and would appreciate it if you both would call a truce at least for the ride home?" She was too exhausted to even contemplate what the hell the cop was doing playing chauffeur. Something didn't feel right about that. She'd been hoping Chris would be there. Sweep her off her feet. Carry her to a waiting limo. Guess not. Her internal rage was now targeted directly at Chris. The nerve of him not coming to get her.

"Sorry, Annie," Luce replied sheepishly.

"Sorry," Andy chimed in. "And uh, we're not going home just yet," he winced on the last part. He could see how tired she was. Knew this wasn't going to go over well.

"Not going home?" Annie stopped and dropped her bag. "Explain or I will not take another step!"

"Seems everyone is gathered over at the Stolz's and the only way I could keep them from coming here was to offer to bring you there."

"Everyone as in everyone who?" Annie asked cautiously.

"Well, uh, everyone." He glanced over at Luce, his eyes pleading for salvation.

"I think, Annie, he means Chris is there, is that what you mean Detective?" Luce smiled sweetly knowing that's exactly what he didn't want her to say.

"Detective?" Annie began tapping her foot. She wasn't sure why but suddenly something about all of this was getting her ire up. Probably the lack of pain meds in her system. They'd warned her that she might have mood swings as she came off them. Mood swings or not, she was completely done with being a victim, or the sorry ass heroine in a late-night movie.

"Who, detective, is waiting for little old Annie Porter to magically appear? Oh wait don't tell me it's my old knight in shining armor, Chris Gregory. Mr. famous author who's secretly been in love with little old me since well since day one. The guy who somehow managed to turn my life into a goddamn made for tv movie complete with murdering nymphomaniac and lying best friend. Hmmm? Hmmmm?

"So yeah, that would be correct," Andy replied, just a bit hesitantly.

"No." Annie suddenly said.

"No? What do you mean no?" Andy sighed. Not going well.

"No, I would like to go home now. Thank you. Just home."

The detective glanced over at Luce to check whether he had an ally or he was on his own here... *yep, on his own.* "OK, Annie. Home it is."

Chapter 17

"Why is there a crowd on my front stoop?" Annie asked the question knowing the answer before it came.

"Sorry, I had to tell them you wanted to go straight home."

"He's there isn't he? It's dark out, but I know he's there. Let me guess. Bill and Jen, Mark Simeon and his wife and oh look, the 5th wheel."

"Really Annie, I am sorry about this, how about I tell everyone to clear out and give you two a little space. Would that help?"

"You tell me! Is this poignant reunion moment a group activity?"

"Ok, I get it. Wait here," the detective replied somewhat sheepishly.

Andy got out of the car and went over to the group anxiously standing around the front stoop of the old brownstone. "Hate to break this up folks, but Annie is needing, no, demanding a little privacy right about now. "

"Sorry, not a chance Detective. I'm not going anywhere and you can tell her that for me!" Chris folded his arms across his chest for emphasis.

"It's OK Chris, you, my friend, can stay. The *rest* of us gotta go."

A decision to reconvene at Bill and Jen's was quickly made, and Andy grabbed Annie's small overnight bags from the car and set them on the sidewalk, walking back over and opening the door for Annie to get out.

"Annie? Ready?" Annie looked up at the big lion-maned NYPD Detective and somehow in that moment realized she'd always been ready. "As I'll ever be, Detective" she replied and gingerly stepped out, using his arm to brace herself. While she was healing well, it would be weeks before the pain subsided fully.

"I've got it from here detective." Annie looked up hearing the all too familiar voice. And sighed. Time to face the proverbial music. At least she had enough mad on to cope with whatever came next.

Saying nothing, he took her arm, and then placed his hand behind her back sending what could only be described as lightning bolts up her spine as he steered her toward the steps and gave a brief wave back at Andy. "We're good Detective. You all can just take off now."

"You okay?" he looked down at Annie, who didn't appear to be okay at all. Even in the dim lamp light he could see she was pale and shaking. He started to think this was so not a good idea.

"Fine. I'm fine," she said quietly.

"Kind of surreal, huh?" Annie muttered. She didn't know whether to laugh or cry. All these years imagining herself finally being with him, only never ever like this. This was *never* how it was supposed to go. The last few weeks were most definitely not what she'd imagined.

"Yeah," he chuckled. "That it is."

"Can we sit?" Annie was suddenly exhausted, and had this crazy urge to just sit and stare at him. She just wanted to take it all in. Before the moment vanished.

"What here? On the stoop?"

"Yes. Right here, right now. Let's do this." Annie tried to sound nonchalant but firm. As if she were in total control. Soooo far from the truth.

She sat on the top stoop, waited for him to join her, then turned to look at him, the streetlight forming a soft glow about his head.

"You were always too good looking for your own good," she began. "But whatever." She waved her hand aimlessly about in the air. "Here's what I need to know. What's my middle name?"

"You don't know?" Chris chuckled softly, trying to lighten the mood. Still a little stunned by the reference to his looks. She of course was more beautiful than ever to him. Same big brown eyes. Same spunk. This was going better than expected, he thought, though his urge to just wrap his arms around her and hug her like crazy was overwhelming. Baby steps he thought, baby steps.

"Of course I know. But do you?" she replied, somewhat exasperated. Keep talking Annie thought, keep talking. *Do not touch, do not touch,* she repeated the mantra in her head as she stared directly at him. She waited for an answer. The need to touch was pretty powerful at that moment. After the party, she had been on cloud nine, waiting for her phone to ring, waiting for that official first date he'd promised.

"OK," he said. "Fair enough. It's Jade. Annie Jade Porter," Chris said softly. Staring right back. Busted.

"That's right. It is. Okay then," she said matter of factly. "Let's go up and I'll take that nap now. When I wake up, if you are still here, you should anticipate that I will have an insatiable appetite." She blushed, knowing immediately that had certainly come out wrong. She had no idea why she was saying any of it. Words just seemed to be pouring out of her mouth on their own.

"Really?" Chris grinned spontaneously, until he let out an "oomph" as Annie elbowed him. "Sorry."

"You do not look sorry."

"OK. Not sorry. It was funny," he was still grinning and it was simply melting her heart.

"Let's just go up." Annie sighed as she realized she was just as hopelessly in love with him as she ever was. But she was too tired to play this out to its conclusion and really did need that nap. There was so much they needed to discuss, so much to put behind them, in order to move ahead.

Chris didn't move from the recliner as Annie slept soundly on the sofa for the next few hours and beyond. He didn't dare touch her or wake her or make a sound. But it was enough for him to just watch her sleep. Annie. His Annie. For now and for always because there would be no way he'd ever ever let go. Unless of course she wasn't interested, but he buried that thought. He'd made that mistake years ago and it cost him. Not again. As she started to stir, he reached for his phone.

"Oh my god what is that smell?" Annie sat up a bit too quickly and winced.

"Well, House Lo Mein, Potstickers, Crab Rangoon and Wonton Soup. Some Braised Garlic Green Beans as well," Chris replied with not just a little pride. "How did I do?"

Annie didn't know whether to laugh or cry or both. All her most favorite Chinese dishes from their late-night study breaks. He remembered every one.

Looking over at him with a sly smile, she replied "Perfect, but where are my chopsticks?"

They ate in companionable silence, as if they did this once a week. Good friends, cross legged on the floor, eating Chinese take-out straight from the box.

"Whatever happens Chris, can we promise to get together once a year and do this?" Annie's voice was teasing, but something caught his attention.

"What, have Chinese for breakfast? Sure. Make it twice a year and you got a deal," he replied lightly not wanting to ruin her mood, wherever it was taking her.

When she'd had her fill, Annie gently placed the chopsticks down on the table and stretched, wincing a bit as she realized how stiff she was.

Looking over at Chris, Annie sighed a bit too loudly. He was actually here. In her apartment. Cross legged on the floor looking like he came straight off a magazine cover. Breathtaking really.

He cocked his head slightly and grinned.

"What?" Annie glared. She knew she'd been caught ogling and feigned indignance seemed a pretty good reaction.

"Nothing. I haven't been this relaxed in years, that's all."

"Oh. I guess I'm happy for you then. Will you tell me something Chris? When did you start writing? I mean photography was your thing. You were so good at it. You weren't writing back in school, I'm pretty sure I would have known if you were wouldn't I? Why was it a big secret? Why is it still?" She really wanted to ask about Ireland, and his deserting her, but for now that could wait. They'd get there.

Chris leaned back on his forearms, and thought for a moment. "I've always loved to write, Annie, but it was something I was afraid of," he paused for a moment. "My dad had dreams of me being an engineer. Photography he didn't see as anything more than a hobby, so I could do it openly. But writing isn't something that he thought was hobby material. So I kept it pretty tightly inside. I used a pen name for my first book, never realizing it would take off like it did. And once C.A. McLain was born, well…"

"I guess now I know why you were always so critical of my writing, you were better than I was all along," Annie teased, hoping to lighten his mood. He suddenly looked a bit sad. "I'm sorry about your dad by the way, I saw your dedication in your last book. At the time I hadn't made the connection though."

"Thanks," Chris replied softly. "At least he finally got to see me for who I was. He loved my books, too. Say, how are your folks doing anyway?" Annie's smile seemed to turn melancholy. "We lost them a few years ago…"

Annie's voice seemed to trail off. "Pile up during the super storm," she paused.

"Oh god Annie, I'd no idea," he stood up suddenly and quickly came around to sit down next to her. He really really needed to give her a hug. Just as he sat, she stood. Nervous and realizing things were going down a very narrow path, she began pacing.

"Annie? You OK?" he realized they were on shaky ground. Which required an abrupt change in mood.

Chris smiled suddenly. "You read my books?"

"What?" Annie glanced over at him. "Of course, but I didn't know they were yours so get that grin off your face. I had no idea you were him. Well, that is, until you wrote about us."

"Does it change things Annie? "

"What do you mean?"

"Nothing. Say Annie, what really happened with Larry? I mean I know you said he was with Nora, but why?"

"You would ask. Well, Larry had a tendency to over-indulge if you get my drift. One too many when I wasn't around. Nora took advantage of that one night. I didn't even know she knew about Larry. I still don't get how she just happened to be there in the same bar as him and hooked up. Water under the bridge now. So, we never got married."

"Too bad for him. I'm sorry if you got hurt. When you returned the gift I wasn't sure what had happened."

"You sent a gift?"

"Yeah but it wasn't sent from a good place, so I'm glad you never opened it."

"Well, let's just say that Larry evidently was not the right guy for me. Nora actually did me a favor that time."

"Had I known I would have given him a gift of his own!" Chris balled his hand into a fist. Annie smiled then, this was her Chris. The guy who made her heart melt. The guy Nora would never ever have.

"I didn't have a girlfriend, you know," Chris sounded a little apologetic.

Annie looked up, eyes wide open now.

"Excuse me?"

"I just wanted to see if I'd get a reaction from you, so when you handed me that wedding invitation asking if I could bring my girlfriend just kind of popped out. I mean after all you were engaged so," Chris realized maybe not all confessions were good for the soul at that point.

Annie's complexion was starting to turn an interesting shade of crimson, and Chris knew this was it. That defining moment. Sink or swim. Go time.

"Forget the girlfriend. Forget Larry, forget the books, forget all of it. You have a car right?"

Annie just nodded suspiciously.

"Listen, leave Luce a note. Let's go for a drive. I want to show you something."

Chapter 18

As Annie stepped down from the stoop, she stopped, turning to face him. "I know you said forget the book, but," Annie chewed on her lower lip, her eyes lowered. Mustering her courage, she looked up at him, determined. "It's just that in the book, Rick tells Max that Jade is in love with him, and Max should just forget her. Was that true? Is that what really happened?"

"They're characters in a book Annie, that's all."

"Oh that's just horse-shit and you know it, Chris!" Annie stomped her foot and then winced. All the pain meds were clearly out of her system now. *Deep breath. OK.* "Listen buddy, I am a 35-year-old spinster recovering from a near death experience and you are just messing with the wrong person here. You took my whole freaking life and put it out there for the world to see in a book. You know it. I know it. So fess up. Now!" Annie didn't really feel quite that sure of herself but after what she'd been through putting her heart on the line didn't seem quite so terrifying.

Chris looked confused. "Your life? That was my life Annie. Mine."

"Soooo you're saying none of it was about me? Maybe you don't think so but those were *my* memories you stole and wrote about."

"Well of course it was about you!" Chris was practically yelling now. The tension between them was palpable and neither seemed to have any control over where this was headed. "How could it not be Annie. My life, your life, it's all one isn't it? How about they were *our* memories. They belonged to both of us. Look. I'm sorry I twisted it all around to suit the story. But it wouldn't have been much of a story if Jade really was in love with Rick, so that's why I made a few changes. I say let's just forget about that and move on. I mean really, it's just a book. Fiction. It's called creative writing for a reason." Chris winced at his own rambling and how dishonest and cowardly this all was. The old fears still lingered. He knew he needed to tell her the truth, but he couldn't.

Annie just stared, open mouthed, not believing what she was hearing.

"Annie. Please, let's just start over. Friends?"

"But. I. Well," Annie could do nothing but stammer. Staring into that sea of emotion in his eyes, seeing an earnest plea. *Wait, a plea for her to be his friend?*

"Nope, not yet." She closed her eyes for a moment and shook her head. "Ireland. We need to put that to rest here and now. You left me sitting on a curb, bags packed and ready to go. Might as well have sliced a hole in my heart. When you came back, and came to see me, I asked you then. You said you didn't want to talk about it. It wasn't important, you said. But it was to me."

"It was all there in the note, Annie. I basically bared my soul to you, remember?"

"What note, Chris? There was no note. No phone call. I left you a zillion voicemails."

"That's not possible. Sam would have told me. He had my phone, I had to take a different one overseas. You're telling me he didn't give you the note?"

She paused, took another deep breath. "No, he didn't. He told me you'd gone, to just let it go and move on. So I packed the rest of my things and came home to NY. I don't know how you really felt back then, between the book and reality it's all a bit blurred."

Annie looked away distantly.

"I did tell you Annie, I did write you a note. I told you to be happy with Sam. Which looking back probably wasn't the right thing to say, was it?"

"Considering it was all a lie, no, it wasn't." There. She'd said it. No taking it back.

"I don't understand. What was a lie?" he sounded curious now.

Annie closed her eyes and one more time, breathed deeply. This is it, now or never.

Opening her eyes, she gazed at him. Every emotion she'd ever felt for Chris came swimming through her eyes. "Just so we're on the same page here, Rick is Sam, and you're Max…"

Chris nodded. "Yeah, kind of obvious."

"In your book, Rick asks Jade how she feels and she lies. Afraid to let Max find out how she felt. Now you didn't include what happened next, but, if you had, you would have made that your excuse to leave without her. Am I right?"

Chris nodded, but remained silent. Watchful.

"Thing is, if Jade is supposed to be me," Annie hesitated then. "If Jade is me, Chris, then you got it wrong. I did NOT tell Sam I had feelings for him. It was Sam that lied to you. And so you left me behind." Annie smiled bittersweetly, and shrugged her shoulders lightly, lowered her gaze, and waited for his reply.

"Son of a bitch!" he exclaimed as it dawned on him.

It seemed they stood there, silent, for a long long time. She could hear him breathing softly, and then just a mumbled curse. She spoke up again, almost rambling. Panic setting in.

"Look Chris, I get it. I do. For you it wasn't real. It was just another book. But for me, well," Annie turned away, hesitating, then took a few steps away from him. Distance. She needed distance.

"Jesus, Annie, what have I just been telling you?" Chris was getting frustrated. He combed his fingers through his hair and took a deep breath. "Seriously. Why can't we just have an honest conversation for once? What the hell is wrong with us?"

Annie stopped, and turned, just as he appeared in one quick step next to her. She looked up but couldn't move. She was frozen. Chris's gaze roamed her face, looking for something, anything to spur him on. His stomach muscles tightened and he felt like he was about to step in front of a speeding train. If what Annie said was true she loved him. Annie loved him. The realization came over him so resolutely he stiffened with rage. At Sam. At himself. For being so damn stupid. All these years wasted. And worst of all, he'd hurt her. Deliberately. He'd abandoned her. Just the image of Annie, sitting alone, waiting, heartbroken. He hadn't had the guts to face her then, and he'd put his trust in the wrong person. He knew now he had only one chance to get her back. And if he blew it, it would be over. There'd never be another chance. He'd been afraid back then. Too scared to admit his feelings. Well not now. He'd have to step up this time and leave no room for doubt.

"Come with me," Chris was suddenly abrupt as he grabbed Annie's hand and began to pull her down the sidewalk. He was going so fast she had to skip a few steps to keep up. Breathless, she tried to slow him down. "Chris where are we going anyway? What's going on? You're pulling me like a rag doll, Chris. Broken Ribs, remember?"

"Damn Annie why didn't you say something!" Chris was angry mostly at himself now, but it didn't matter. "Bruised not broken, but hell I'm so sorry, Annie."

Chris slowed down, relaxing his stride and his grip, but said nothing as he gently pulled her along. "Where's your car?" he asked abruptly. She silently pointed, her chin quivering nervously. "Give me the keys, and stop chewing on your lip." Annie looked up in surprise. Her eyes wide, she handed him the keys. Chris opened the passenger door. "Get in" he said as he firmly guided her into the seat. He strode around the front of the car, and slipping in next to her, he grabbed the seat lever and pushed his seat all the way back. "They don't make cars any smaller than this do they, huh Annie?" Annie looked over in disbelief. All this chaotic drama surrounding them and he's cracking stupid short jokes.

At this point Annie was simply overwhelmed by swirling emotions. She had no idea what he was thinking, or why they were in her car, or why he seemed so suddenly different. One minute charming, the next ferocious. Glancing up at him, she could see he was in ferocious mode again. Clenched jaw, the angry eyes. It was just too much. She felt every nerve ending in her body. Her breaths became shallow, her heart racing.

"Where are we going, Chris?" Her voice was shaky, barely a whisper. Chris said nothing. Not a word. He wasn't sure whether to laugh or cry or scream. All this time he'd been desperately waiting for the chance to make Annie see that he was the one for her. He'd planned on how to slowly rekindle their friendship, and from there, take that next step. Tread lightly. Don't spook her. Especially with the horror of the last few weeks. His jaw clenched tighter as he realized not only had she been in danger from an old jealousy, he'd been a victim as well.

Never did he once suspect he'd been played for a fool for so long. Though Sam had never come close to putting him or Annie in danger, what he'd done was unforgiveable. He'd known Sam all his life. They'd been inseparable. And he'd betrayed him. Just as he'd betrayed Martha. Annie loved him. He saw it in her eyes just moments ago. He hadn't imagined it all those years ago. His memories weren't distorted. He had simply been too afraid to face his own feelings and grabbed at any straw to back off. Sam had given him a good reason, and he'd jumped on it. He wouldn't make that same mistake twice. He was older, maybe a little wiser now, but most certainly more confident. And this time he would take control, and Annie would be his. OK maybe not his, and maybe he'd never have control, it is Annie after all, but he'd at least try.

"You're not on drugs are you?" Annie gave a nervous laugh, because at this point, she had no idea but she was in fact just a little terrified.

"No, oh my god Annie, no, oh crap I'm sorry," Chris reached over and took Annie's hand. "I'm not on drugs and I'm not angry at you and I haven't lost my mind even though I'm acting like a lunatic. So bear with me just a little longer and you'll see. Okay?" Chris sounded sincere, and Annie just quietly nodded.

######

"They're gone!" Luce yelled from the living room. Running into the hall, she grabbed Andy's arm. "Did you hear me? They're gone! Her car's gone. He's got Annie and he's taken her somewhere. Maybe we were wrong. Oh god!" Luce was panicked.

Andy shook his head and taking Luce's hand off his arm gently, he held on firmly. "Luce, they have things to talk about. They need some alone time."

"What if he was behind all this?" Luce persisted. He saw the pleading look in her eyes, knew she needed reassurance.

"Luce, we have the perp. She confessed. I've spent a lot of time with Chris. Listen to me, Luce. It's okay." His voice was soothing, none of the sarcasm usually present. He knew right now she needed him to comfort her. He wasn't sure how.

"It's called love, Luce." He couldn't stop the cynical tone from creeping back in. "Have you ever actually felt anything Luce? For a person, not a bank account?"

He knew it was the wrong thing to say, and quickly apologized. "Sorry, out of line. I know you're worried. But there's no need. Did you see the way he looked at her? The way she looked at him?"

"Kind of the way you guys ogle each other, eh?" Bill's voice boomed behind them. "She left a note for you Luce," Bill added with a grin. "They went for a drive," he continued on. "Sorry had to read it."

They both turned to him, startled. Looking back at each other, their expressions horrified, they backed away from each other.

"I'm going home now," Luce stammered out.

"Me too," Andy muttered and gave Luce a shuttered glance. "After you?"

Chapter 19

They'd been driving for almost an hour. In total silence. Annie had thought about turning on the radio, but one glance at Chris's face and she opted not to. He still looked angry. No, maybe not angry. But there was a swirl of emotions on his face she couldn't read. Annie gazed out the window as Chris pulled onto a small narrow road. It ran directly parallel to the water, and between the houses, Annie could see the crisp blue waves and strips of sand. Chris slowed down, and put on his turn signal. Up ahead she spotted a driveway, barely visible among the tall leafy trees that lined it. As they turned in, she gasped. There it stood. A beautiful white colonial, with a neat circular drive out front. In the center, a lush green lawn dotted with flower beds. And lining the drive, low white picket fencing. The house itself wasn't small, but it was charming. And she knew without a doubt that the back overlooked the water.

"Chris?" Annie's voice was curious has he turned the engine off. "Whose house is this? Where exactly are we?"

He turned and smiled at her. A slow, seductive smile that made her toes curl and her heart race. The tension in his face had dissipated. "You'll see," he replied softly. He got out and came around to open her door. Taking her hand, he gently pulled her out onto the drive this time and looked down at her. "Ready?" He asked, still smiling.

"Honestly, I don't know. I'm so confused, Chris." Annie looked pleadingly at him.

"Well, you won't be for much longer." He held onto his resolve, though her eyes were big and luminous, and he felt like crumbling.

Still holding her hand, gently this time, pulling her along, they walked up to the entryway. Annie couldn't speak. She'd never had a panic attack, but she was sure she was about to. This was her dream house. Seriously. Exactly as she'd envisioned it. Exactly.

Annie waited for Chris to ring the bell, but he made no move to do so. He stood looking around the front as if taking it all in. Then he reached into his pocket and pulled out a key. Annie looked at the key in his hand, and felt a lump in her throat. He didn't live here. This couldn't be his house. But the key fit neatly in the lock, and as she stood, dumbfounded, the front door opened. Stepping into the foyer, Chris placed his hand on the small of her back, guiding her in. He felt her shoulders stiffen, and for an instant wondered if he'd been wrong. But there was no turning back.

Annie's eyes widened in surprise. The house was empty. Not a stitch of furniture. "Chris? Whose house is this?" Annie's voice was a little more in control now.

"Mine." He replied quickly, grinning.

"You live here? But there's nothing here."

"I didn't say I lived here, yet, but I do own it."

Annie gazed around, her eyes taking it all in. "It's perfect," she whispered. *Truly perfect.* The living room was straight back past the oak stairway. It was sunken, with broad steps leading down. A beehive fireplace in the corner gave it a warm appeal, and the broad picture windows afforded a spectacular view of the coastline. She had a sudden pang of jealously and tried to hold her thoughts back, but didn't know if she could.

"More. I need to see more."

Chris chuckled, "Right this way ma'am."

"And don't call me ma'am, as in ever," Annie elbowed him for good measure. "You keep doing that I'll have a few busted ribs too!" Chris exclaimed.

"You get what you give Chris!"

"OK, kitchen."

Annie stopped in the arched entry to the kitchen to take it in. It was truly spectacular. Floor to ceiling white cupboards with intricate brass pulls. The massive stone topped island in the center. 8-burner Gas Cooktop. It was her dream kitchen, no doubt. "Better move on, this is too great for words," Annie sighed.

"Onward and upward Madam!" Chris laughed as that earned him a stomp on his foot. He was completely relaxed now. Watching Annie tour the home gave him absolute certainty that this was her home. Her place. She belonged here. And it was evident from her every reaction as they walked through the house.

Up the stairs they went, down a short hall and through a set of French doors, to the Master Suite. Complete with a wall of floor to ceiling windows, and a slider opening to a full deck, with stunning views of the water.

Annie stepped outside, and stood at the deck rail, staring for a moment. Gathering her thoughts. Struggling with her emotions.

"It couldn't be more perfect, Chris," she said in a dangerously quiet voice, still staring out at the water.

Somehow he knew she didn't want him to say a word. He knew there was more coming.

"Why, Chris, why do *you* have a house like this? This should be my house damnit. I've worked my butt off for 10 years and all I have to show for it is a dumpy little apartment. And let's not forget how you laughed about my vision, you thought my picket fences were silly! What was it you once said? Only grannies lived in houses with picket fences?" Annie's temper was flaring, and she could do nothing to stop it. Here she was in her dream house, with her dream lover, but they weren't hers. They never would be. She turned away for a moment, trying to stop the inevitable tears, but it was no use. Why couldn't she just, for once, get what she wanted?

Seeing her turn away and knowing he had one shot at this, and only one, he quickly swung Annie around to face him, her back toward the rail. Placing both hands on either side of her, caging her in, he looked at her, and saw the tears brimming in her eyes.

"Oh, Annie," he whispered gently, "please, don't cry," and he gently wiped a tear with his thumb. "Please." Chris's voice was hushed, and Annie thought, incredibly sexy.

"I can't help it," Annie's reply barely made it out. She couldn't speak now. Her whole world was in a free-fall.

Chris took a breath, *now or never* he thought.

"I bought it for you, Annie. For us."

The words were barely out of his mouth when he leaned in closer.

The realization hit Annie like a freight train.

"Us?" Annie whispered in surprise.

A small smile played on his lips. "Yeah. Us."

Annie held her breath and watched as the face she'd known and loved and wanted for so long drew closer. His lips were slightly parted, and she knew without a doubt what was going to happen. And was powerless to stop it. She wanted this so badly it hurt. And the moment his lips brushed hers, she was a goner. Annie thought she'd died and gone to heaven. Her whole body felt like it was being bombarded with sensations she'd never, ever had. As he deepened the kiss, his tongue began the slow exploration she'd fantasized about since she'd first laid eyes on him. Annie couldn't think anymore. Not a coherent thought could be found as her world slowly dissolved away and she let herself ride the waves of emotions that had taken over. She was in another place now. A place so perfect she could die happy right then and there. But it was far from over. His hands, which he'd so gently placed on her shoulders, had begun a slow, downward journey. Caressing her body with just a light feathery touch, making her shudder with each new stop. She could feel herself sliding down and reached her arms around his neck to hold herself up. She felt his heat, his hunger and wanted him to devour her, right there. She needed to be closer, she couldn't seem to get enough of him.

As suddenly as it had started, it was over. He pulled back, lifting his head and turning it away. He pulled her close, leaning his chin on her forehead. His breathing was labored, and he struggled to maintain control. "Annie, god I'm sorry Annie, but we need to stop. We need to talk."

"Talk later," Annie pleaded, her voice barely audible.

"No, Annie," Chris replied hoarsely. "Now." He let his arms slide down and stepped away. Awkwardly, he ran his fingers through his hair, struggling to find the right words. Annie felt a sudden coldness sweep over her. Though he hadn't moved that far from her, it was as if he'd left her completely.

"Chris, please, tell me. Wait. Don't. Oh my god, there's already someone else. You bought it for us and then you met her. Everyone, and I mean everyone, said you were single, including you. Seriously do NOT play me for the fool."

"Don't be absurd Annie," Chris laughed.

Annie was beginning to feel her control slip away, as it suddenly dawned on her that none of this was her fault. Not one bit. And she felt her insecurity fade as the anger built up. Mustering her strength, she pulled away to face him. "I can't do this anymore Chris. Now or never." Chris chuckled at her choice of words. *Yep, now or never.*

"Don't you dare laugh! I have a right to my life. And I'm not wasting another minute on you unless you come clean with me. A minute ago I would have sworn you felt for me what I've always felt for you. Then suddenly you're all "let's talk" and I'm thinking uh uh. No way. I want the truth, Chris. All of it. I deserve that much. Start with when. *When* did you buy this house?"

Looking down at her upturned face, seeing the anger and the passion swirling in her eyes, Chris took a deep breath. He locked his gaze on hers, and placing both hands on her shoulders, perhaps to hold her in place, he went for broke. "Right after the 4th. I knew then that what was between us was real, and lasting. It had endured all of our screw ups. Mark and I were out on his boat, and when I saw this house, I knew I had to buy it. For you. For us."

"What you felt just now, Annie, can't come close to what I felt. What I've always felt. I told you, I wrote it all down in the book. Hell it was all in the note I left for you with Sam. I wrote that you should be happy with Sam. That I didn't want my feelings to get in the way of yours. I never thought for even a second that he didn't give it to you. When I said that the book was just fiction, OK that was a lie. I couldn't seem to tell you the truth. I was too afraid. Afraid that you didn't want me. But everything I wrote, as far as Max Colby goes, was the truth. Every word. It's you Annie, it's always been you."

"Go on," Annie was totally lost in the moment now. Hopelessly grinning from ear to ear.

"More?"

"Yep, more please."

"OK. Here it is. I loved you the first minute I saw you, and never stopped. When Sam told me you were in love with him, I thought I'd die from the pain. It hurt so bad I wanted to kill him. He convinced me to back off, go to Ireland alone, so I did. I thought maybe we could salvage our friendship if I did. How could I have known it was all a lie?" He looked away for a moment, gathering his thoughts.

"When I think back on how I must have hurt you, it brings up so much pain. I wouldn't hurt you for the world. You *are* my world, don't you see that? When I thought I lost you," he paused running his hands over his face, "I thought I'd die. It would have been my fault, don't you see?"

Annie shook her head furiously, tears pouring down her face. They were uncontrollable, but they weren't tears of sadness. It was pure joy. She reached up with one hand and gently laid it on his cheek. "It wasn't your fault, Chris, any of it. Nora is the only one to blame for putting me in danger. She's always been like a bad shadow for me. I just never realized how crazy she really was. So some of this is my fault, I suppose," Annie sighed.

"How so?" Chris asked curiously.

"Well, I guess I lied too, all those years ago, because I told her I had a thing for Sam, to keep her away from you."

Chris chuckled. "You did, huh?"

Annie blushed. "I did. I knew if she thought I wanted you she'd go after you."

"What makes you think I'd have gone for her? Give me a little credit, Annie." Annie smiled at that. He had a point.

"But, you shouldn't have let him interfere, Chris. You should have told me yourself how you felt. And I guess I shouldn't have trusted him either.

So, we're both at fault. In fact," Annie's face suddenly looked somber, "If I hadn't lied to Nora, maybe Martha would still be here."

Chris shook his head, "No way, Annie, you can't put that on you. Whether or not the drugs were tampered with, Martha chose to take them. And Nora poisoned her with them. What's done is done, Annie, we can't change it. Can't fix it."

"But we're here now, and we can fix this, I mean us, can't we? I've changed, I know, but you're older too, right? I mean, I," Annie stammered now, afraid of the worst.

He drew her back to him, enfolding her in his arms. Holding her tightly as he'd needed to do since he first laid eyes on her getting out of the car. Knowing she was safe. Here. With him.

"Only one way to fix it Annie. And I won't settle for anything less. If we do this, we do it all the way. This house, kids. You and me till death do us part. Got it?" He was breathless and tense, waiting to see if he'd pushed too far, too soon.

He leaned his head back and fixed his gaze on hers and hoped.

Annie's mouth twitched slightly, and she chuckled softly. "Kids, hmm?" And as she gazed back at the face she'd dreamed about for half her life, she smiled broadly. "Maybe we should have that first date and then we'll see…" she whispered as her mouth reached for his.

Annie and Chris both jumped at the sudden eruption of laughter and cheers. Looking over at the beach, there they were. The gang of 6, looking just about as happy and smug as any friends could.

"Figured you were here my friend," Mark called out. He'd known as soon as they found the note where Chris had brought Annie. And couldn't be happier for them both. Just what his best writer needed. Happy wife, happy life, and more books on the way…

****

About the Author

When she's not making up stories to entertain herself with, MJ Miller can be found looking for ways to beat the southwestern heat. Usually traveling north to just about anywhere. Hobbies include baking chocolate things, eating chocolate things, and using a treadmill to remove the evidence. As the mother of two grown women she loves to write about daughters and sisters and all the tangled-up relationships they tend to have, always believing the road to a happy life is filled with laughter. She and her incredible husband reside in the balmy desert southwest with their Mensa qualifying cat, Darwin.

Other Books by MJ Miller

The Christoph Curse

For Sarah Bennett, things had gone completely out of her control. Suddenly finding herself mother to her orphaned niece, Addy, Sarah is thrust into a strange and dangerous world. To keep her and Addy safe, she reluctantly takes a job with Addy's enigmatic uncle, Sam, who apparently is the victim of sabotage and linked to a foreign government in alleged turmoil. Not to mention the fact that the nanny she hired is psychic and someone is trying to scare her to death. When had her life become a damn soap opera? Things like this weren't supposed to happen. Not to Sarah, anyway. Sarah must battle her own demons, grief and the threats against her as well as fight off her instant and combustible attraction to Sam if she's going to survive and create a new life for her and Addy. But Sam's got other ideas. And secrets that could change Sarah's life forever.

Made in the USA
Columbia, SC
01 August 2020